The Finders-Keepers Rule

A Maryellen Mystery

by Jacqueline Dembar Greene

★ American Girl®

Special thanks to Judy Woodburn

Published by American Girl Publishing
Copyright © 2016 American Girl

16 17 18 19 20 21 LEO 11 10 9 8 7 6 5 4 3 2 1

Cover image by Juliana Kolesova

The following individuals and organizations have given permission to use
images incorporated into the cover design: Daytona Beach postcard image in
lower panel, courtesy of Lake Country Discovery Museum; Daytona Beach
bandshell, © iStock.com/Jason Ganser; elements of border design, © iStock.
com/Maljuk; background pattern on back cover, © kirstypargeter/Crestock.

Cataloging-in-Publication Data available from the Library of Congress.

To Jennifer Hirsch,
confidence booster, colleague, friend

Beforever™

The adventurous characters you'll meet in
the BeForever books will spark your curiosity
about the past, inspire you to find your voice
in the present, and excite you about your future.
You'll make friends with these girls as you share
their fun and their challenges. Like you, they are
bright and brave, imaginative and energetic,
creative and kind. Just as you are, they are
discovering what really matters: Helping others.
Being a true friend. Protecting the earth.
Standing up for what's right. Read their stories,
explore their worlds, join their adventures.
Your friendship with them will BeForever.

TABLE *of* CONTENTS

chapter 1

Dancing to the Beat

MARYELLEN HELD HER arms out in mid-air, pretending she was dancing with a partner. *To the right, to the left, step back, step front,* she urged her clumsy feet. *Right, left, back, front.* "You're such a cool dancer," she said aloud to her imaginary date. "You haven't stepped on my toes more than ten times!"

Maryellen's older sister Carolyn let out a giggle. Then she stopped smiling and turned stern again. "That's enough clowning around," she said. "You must listen to the beat of the music, and do all the steps without stopping to think about each one. Otherwise, you'll never be ready to Rock Around the Clock with me."

That was exactly what Maryellen was worried about. Winter vacation from school was half over, and the annual dance near the famous Daytona Beach clock tower was just four days away. When she was younger, Maryellen had been content to watch from the sidelines as her older sisters danced with their dates, skirts swirling as they moved in time to the music. Maryellen had loved just being on the plaza amid all the hubbub: the holiday lights twinkling, the band's music blaring from the stage, the people on the dance floor rocking and rolling. This year, though, she wanted to be part of the excitement. She wanted to dance—and that was turning out to be a whole lot harder than it looked. Carolyn had been patiently trying to help Maryellen learn the rock 'n' roll steps, but somehow Maryellen's feet kept getting tangled up.

I can do it, she told herself. She took a deep breath and stood taller. Carolyn turned her transistor radio up a bit louder. Maryellen speeded up her movements to match the song's fast beat. No sooner did she step to the right than she missed the cue to step back.

"Okay, Ellie," Carolyn said, snapping off the radio. "Try it with me." Carolyn rested her right hand on Maryellen's waist, and Maryellen placed her left hand on Carolyn's shoulder. Then the girls clasped their free hands and held them out to the side. Carolyn walked Maryellen slowly through the steps.

When she danced with the music on again, Maryellen thought she was finally matching the steps to the beat. "Much better!" Carolyn told her. "Now you need to make those steps smoother. Let your body move with the beat, too. You'll need to practice that on your own. I've got to get over to the band shell to pick up some posters. I volunteered to hang them up around town."

Carolyn disappeared into the kitchen and returned a moment later with a roll of tape. She slipped it into her bag and strode to the door. "See you later, Ellie." As the screen door slammed behind her, Carolyn called back over her shoulder. "Practice!"

Of course I will, Maryellen thought. She waited for a slow song on the radio to end and stood ready to try the swing dance again as soon as the disc jockey played a rock 'n' roll song. In a moment, she heard him introduce a fun song with a fast, heavy beat: "Later Alligator" by Bobby Charles. Maryellen had barely managed a few steps when her younger sister, Beverly, interrupted.

"I'll dance with you," she offered. "After all, I do take dancing lessons."

"No, thanks," Maryellen said, trying not to sound annoyed. Beverly never missed a chance to show how good she was at dancing. "First of all, you take ballet. That's nothing like rock 'n' roll. Second of all, I need a partner who can lead. I'm the one who has to follow."

"I could learn it faster than you," Beverly taunted her.

Maryellen knew her little sister was probably right. By now, she had lost her rhythm. She felt relieved when the radio station took a break for commercials.

"Hey, all you cool cats out there," an announcer said. "Be sure to head to the band shell next Saturday night at seven sharp. It's the annual Daytona Beach Dance. Time to Rock Around the Clock! Be there or be square!"

"I wanna dance, too," said Maryellen's little brother Tom. He was just five, but he was what Maryellen's father called "a bundle of perpetual motion." Tom wiggled and waved his arms, singing the jingle from a toothpaste commercial. Their old dachshund, Scooter, woke up from one of his many naps and started howling along. In the kitchen, Maryellen's three-year-old brother, Mikey, was having a temper tantrum because Mom wouldn't let him have a cookie. Mikey didn't like to hear the word "no" unless he was saying it.

"That's it," Maryellen complained. "I can't practice around here." She stepped into the kitchen and announced, "I'm heading to the beach."

"Check in with Joan when you get there," Maryellen's mother said, trying to talk above Mikey's fussing. "And let her know when you leave."

Maryellen's sister Joan, who was now Mrs. Jerry Ross, was working at a food stand on the beach. This was another reason Maryellen liked being at the beach. It was neat to hang around with Joan and Jerry and hear about what they were doing. They were so busy that Maryellen didn't get to see them much.

She rolled her bike from the garage and pedaled off. The ocean was several blocks from her house, but it was an easy ride. Maryellen cruised along Ocean Avenue, passing by the wide walled plaza on her left. Over its high walls, she could see the top of the open band shell and one face of the tall clock tower that rose above everything. She breathed in the familiar scent of salty air and caught a few quick glimpses of blue waves rolling in to shore.

Just past the plaza, she turned left and coasted down Main Street, which led directly to the beach. Maryellen thought the best part of school vacation was getting to spend time here. Gliding down Main Street, she could see the length of the wooden pier that jutted out into the ocean, high above the water on tall wooden pilings. Men cast fishing lines over the railing. Couples walked hand in hand toward the restaurant at the end of the pier, the men wearing loose-fitting tropical shirts and the women in pastel-colored cotton dresses that billowed in the breeze.

Maryellen kept to the side of the road as cars cruised slowly past her, their windows open to the air. She looked with longing at a shiny green convertible filled with laughing teenagers. The top was down, and the girls protected their hairdos with bright scarves. Music blared from the car's radio.

Maryellen glided under the stone arches of a stairway that led from the pier to the sandy beach. As soon as her bike wobbled onto the hard-packed sand, she hopped off and walked it along the beach, leaving Main Street and the pier behind her. The green convertible had pulled into a row of cars parked right on the sand, and the teens were climbing out of the car. Nearby, people stretched out on beach blankets or sat on webbed chairs. The winter holidays brought lots of tourists from colder states up north, and the beach was crowded. Children splashed in the water until they scurried, shivering, to their parents, who bundled them in giant towels. Out on the water, a flock of pelicans bobbed on the waves, their long bills protruding over the pouches full of fish that bulged at their throats. Seagulls circled overhead, their shrill cries piercing the air. To Maryellen, the scene felt like a giant party. Even the birds seemed to be in on the fun.

It was a short walk to Sandy's Beach Hut, the food stand on the beach where Joan worked. As she approached, Maryellen could hear a radio on the counter playing "Shake, Rattle and Roll." In the

shadow of the shack's blue awning, Maryellen saw
her sister dancing with her husband, Jerry. Just as
the song was ending, Joan leaned back against Jerry's
arm. On the final beat, he flipped her over expertly.
Joan landed on her feet in the soft sand, her arms
outstretched. Her boss, Sandy, applauded.

"Wow!" Maryellen exclaimed, leaning her bike
against the side of the shack. "I don't think I'll ever
be able to do anything that fancy."

"Sure you will, Ellie, if you keep practicing,"
Jerry said. He reached for Maryellen's hand, held it
up high, and gave her a dizzying twirl. She giggled
with delight.

Maryellen still couldn't quite believe that Jerry
was her brother-in-law. He and Joan had begun
dating when Joan was in high school, and they had
gotten married only a few months ago. Jerry was the
most handsome man Maryellen knew, and possibly
the bravest. He had trained as a diver and served in
the Navy during the Korean War. He once confided

to Maryellen that he had gone on secret underwater missions. That seemed scary, and even more exciting than the television shows and movies Maryellen loved to watch—because it was real.

A couple draped in beach towels stepped up to the shack. Joan went behind the counter, pulled two icy bottles of Coca-Cola out of the cooler, and popped off the caps on a bottle opener attached to the side of the stand.

"Keep dancing," Sandy said after the couple left. "Maybe you'll attract a few customers who'll order something besides a nickel soda." He lifted a conch shell from a bucket, revealing the pink underside of its spiky white shell. "I don't know why people aren't lined up to order this delicacy."

Maryellen felt her lips puckering at the thought of eating the rubbery shellfish Sandy pried from the shells. She couldn't understand why anyone liked conch—even fried. She looked up at a chalkboard sign that hung under a plastic Christmas wreath next to Sandy's counter. The sign read, "Daytona's Best Fried Conch."

"Most people want a hot dog," Maryellen said. "Maybe you should have that on the menu."

"Hot dogs?" Sandy frowned, his thin gray hair flopping down over his bushy eyebrows. "Why, you can get those anyplace. But fresh conch—that's a Daytona Beach specialty. Jerry and his pal Skip deliver them right from the ocean to my stand." Sandy emptied the conch shells from the bucket. "I think Skip's glad to have you working with him. I just wish I could use more of these."

Jerry smiled. "Skip wishes you could use more, too," he said. "He keeps complaining that he's barely making enough money to put gas in his boat tank."

Joan turned up the volume on the radio and held out her hands to Jerry. Just as they were about to start dancing again, a muscular young man in a T-shirt and shorts came jogging up the beach, his blond hair bleached nearly white by the sun.

"Jerry!" he called out.

"Hey, Skipper," Jerry said. "What's up?"

Maryellen had heard about Jerry's diving partner but hadn't met him before. She was about to greet him, when Skip tapped Jerry's arm. "Let's get a move on," he said. "Tank wants to talk about the next dive. And he's in a hurry. We'd better get back to the dinghy before he blows his top."

Maryellen looked in the direction from which Skip had come. She could just make out a figure standing next to a small rowboat beached on the sand. Out in the water, past the end of the pier, a larger boat with a covered cabin bobbed next to a red-and-white buoy. Maryellen knew that bigger boats would scrape bottom in the shallow water if they came in too close to the beach. Jerry and Skip used the smaller dinghy to bring the conch to shore for the beachside shacks and restaurants.

"So who's Tank, and what's he hired you for?" Sandy asked.

"We're counting fish," Skip answered after a brief pause. "Tank's a professor at the university. He needed a couple of divers to figure out how many kinds of fish are just offshore. He's a tough boss, and the pay's lousy. The sooner I'm done with it, the better." He chuckled and added, "I'm glad I'm not in school, or I'd have to take orders from guys like him all the time."

Jerry's shoulders stiffened, and Maryellen could see that he didn't appreciate his friend's attitude about school. She knew how hard it was for Jerry and Joan to hold down jobs and go to classes at the university, and how important finishing their education was to each of them. But Jerry was easygoing and didn't like to argue.

"Let's get going then," was all he said. He and Skip set off toward the dinghy.

"Jerry didn't even say good-bye," Joan complained. "Skip's right about one thing: Tank really is demanding, and the work has kept Jerry awfully busy."

Maryellen nodded sympathetically. "Does he really have to dive for conch *and* work for Tank?"

"Jerry doesn't like me to brag about it," Joan said, lowering her voice a bit, "but what he's doing for Tank is more than just a job. Tank teaches courses in oceanography—that's studying the ocean, and everything in it. Jerry is the best student in the class, and an experienced diver, so when the professor needed a crew for his research project, he asked Jerry first. Then Jerry told Tank about Skip and his boat, and they both got a job."

Sandy held out the dented bucket that had held the conch. "Your big brother ran off so fast, he forgot the pail," he said. "How 'bout returning it for me?"

"Sure!" Maryellen said, taking the bucket. She liked the idea of having a big brother—which, in a way, Jerry was, now that he had married Joan—and she liked being able to help him out. She trotted off toward the boat, swinging the pail at her side.

As Maryellen neared the pier, a strange clicking

noise coming from farther up the beach caught her attention. She turned toward the sound and saw two men walking slowly along the sand, their heads bent over some sort of machine. One man was dressed in plaid Bermuda shorts, a neatly tucked pink polo shirt, and leather dress shoes with thin socks. He looked odd, dressed like that on the beach, and the machine he held looked even odder. It reminded Maryellen of her mother's new Hoover vacuum, but instead of a brush, it had a large, flat disc at its bottom end. Instead of the vacuum's hum, this machine was giving off buzzing clicks. At first, the sounds came slowly, spaced far apart. Then the clicks came rapid-fire: *clickety, clickety, clickety, clickety!*

The second man walked alongside the machine, holding a pitchfork with bent tines. He was dressed in work pants, work boots, and a dark green shirt. Maryellen thought he looked about Jerry's age, but unlike Jerry, he was short, and built like a barrel.

Curious, Maryellen walked over to get a closer

look. The older man looked up and gave her a friendly smile. "I'll bet you've never seen one of these before," he said.

"You're right about that," Maryellen answered. "What is that thing?"

The man tapped his knuckles against the machine's handle. "What you are looking at here, little miss, is a scientific breakthrough. You hear those clicks?"

Maryellen nodded vigorously.

"The faster they go, the closer the Buckley Metal Detector is to some metal object buried under the sand," the man said. "This device is going to be a huge success, which is why I've bought the company and named it after myself."

"Wow!" Maryellen exclaimed. "Then you must be Mr. Buckley."

"Indeed I am," the man said. "I'm Atherton Buckley, and this is my assistant, Pete Jones."

Maryellen introduced herself and then asked,

"Have you found anything yet?"

"I have," Mr. Buckley responded. "When the detector is crackling, Pete uses his clam digger to scoop under the sand and see what's buried there. So far this week, I've found some coins, a silver ID bracelet, and a wedding ring."

Maryellen leaned forward to see the dial on the machine.

"Of course," Mr. Buckley went on, "I've turned in the items that people might be looking for—especially the wedding ring. So I'm embarrassed to say I've only earned thirty seven cents this week!" After a moment, he leaned in and lowered his voice. "But just between us, I'm hoping to find far more interesting things. Who knows what treasures lie buried beneath the sand?"

At the word "treasure," Maryellen felt a little flush of excitement. "Ooh," she said. "Buried treasure, like in the movies!" When the movie *Treasure Island* came to their town a few months earlier, she and her friend Davy, who lived next door, had gone to see it three times. Then they'd borrowed the book from the school library and read it to each other, acting out their favorite parts. Just thinking about buried treasure brought back the magical way she'd felt sitting in the darkened theater, nibbling on popcorn, completely lost in the adventures of a young boy, Jim Hawkins, as he battled pirates on his search for hidden treasure. What Maryellen had loved best was that Jim had been no older than Maryellen or Davy, but he was the hero of the story, and everyone listened to his ideas. That was just how Maryellen wanted to be: a hero with ideas that everyone agreed were good. For a long time after the movie left town, she and Davy had talked about it, and Maryellen couldn't stop imagining herself in the scenes.

"Well, almost," Mr. Buckley said, smiling.

Maryellen wished she could follow the men and their machine to see what else they might discover, but the weight of the bucket in her hand reminded her of why she'd walked toward the pier. "Thanks for showing me your metal detector," she said. "But I really need to get this bucket over to my brother-in-law." She lifted the pail and gestured toward the dinghy where Jerry and the two other men were standing.

Buckley and Pete looked at the dinghy with interest. "I noticed there's been a dive boat trolling out there for a few weeks," Mr. Buckley said. "What ever are they doing?"

Maryellen stood up straighter, glad that she knew the answer. "They're studying fish for the university."

"Fascinating," Mr. Buckley said, rubbing his chin thoughtfully. Then he let out a laugh. "I just hope they aren't studying sharks! There are plenty of those out there."

"I sure hope they don't see any," Maryellen said. "Even more, I hope no sharks see them! Well, I'd better go. Good luck with your treasure hunting."

chapter 2
A Strange Warning

MARYELLEN RAN ALONG the water's
edge towards the dinghy, which had been pulled
onto the damp sand near the pier. Jerry, Skip, and
a third man wearing dark sunglasses and a blue-
and-white bandanna were bent over a large sheet of
paper spread on the wooden seat of the small boat.
As she got closer, Maryellen could see that the paper
was some kind of map, and that Jerry was writing
notes on it.

Maryellen loved maps, and geography was one
of her best subjects at school. She dashed up to get a
better look, but what she was able to see over Jerry's
shoulder seemed nothing like the maps in her fifth-
grade classroom. This map was blue and covered
with shapes like wavy circles, one inside the next.

There were red dots in various spots, each with a scribbled note in handwriting too tiny to make out. For a moment, Maryellen forgot about the bucket in her hand.

"What kind of map is that, Jerry?" she asked.

Jerry looked up. "What?" he asked, seeming startled. "Oh, it's just a navigational map for sailors. It helps us see where we are when we're out on the ocean, and how deep the water is in different places."

"What do the circles—" Maryellen began.

Before she could finish her question, the man wearing sunglasses stood and gathered up the map. Maryellen could see that he was older than Jerry and Skip, and seemed to be in charge. "Well," he said briskly, "we ought to get back out on the water." He rolled the map up with a few quick twists of his wrists and slipped it into a storage tube.

Maryellen remembered the bucket and held it out to Jerry. "You forgot this at Sandy's."

"Thanks, Ellie," Jerry said, taking the pail from her. He reached over and tugged her ponytail. "Now I owe you a favor."

Maryellen shaded her eyes from the sun's glare and looked toward the large boat bobbing at anchor. Going out on the boat would be even better than riding in a convertible. "Any chance you might take me for a ride?" she asked. "That would—"

The third man interrupted. "Sorry, kiddo, but that's a working boat," he said, not sounding sorry at all. "It's not for joyrides."

Maryellen studied his face to see if perhaps he was teasing, but she didn't see a hint of a smile.

"This is Tank," Jerry told Maryellen. "Tank, this is my sister-in-law, Maryellen."

"Nice to meet you," Tank responded, but he had already turned away and was tucking the map tube under a seat in the dinghy. He looked toward Jerry and made a curt waving motion with his hand. "Let's get going."

Maryellen couldn't help feeling a little put out. Even when Jerry and Joan were working, they at least had time to be friendly. She was about to say good-bye and head back to her bike when she saw Tank zero in on something farther up the beach.

"What do we have here?" he muttered to Skip and Jerry. He removed his sunglasses and squinted.

Maryellen turned to see what had gotten Tank's attention. Then she smiled. "That's Mr. Atherton Buckley and his helper, Pete Jones. I just met them on my way over here," Maryellen said, pleased to have a way to feel helpful again.

Tank's gaze followed the two men as they zig-zagged along the beach. "What are they doing nosing around?"

"They've got a metal detector that finds things hidden under the sand," Maryellen explained. "When they find something, the machine clicks like crazy." She made rapid clicking noises with her tongue. "Then they start digging. They already found a wedding ring and a silver bracelet and some loose change."

"I've read about that technology," Tank mused. "I didn't know any of the machines were light enough to carry around." His eyes narrowed. "If anyone could afford equipment like that, it would have to be Atherton Buckley. "

"Do you know him?" Jerry asked.

"I sure know *about* him," Tank said. "He lives in a stone mansion on Halifax Avenue. You know the one with the ship's cannon on the front lawn? That's his place. It backs up to the river. He's even got his own dock."

"I've biked past that a hundred times," Maryellen said. "I never imagined I'd meet the person who lives there. He must be really rich!"

Skip gave a low whistle. "I think everyone who lives on Halifax made a mint in some big industry."

"Buckley made his money in railroads," Tank said. "He spends a fortune collecting things salvaged from shipwrecks—like the cannon."

"Why's he scouring the beach for lost pocket change?" Maryellen wondered aloud.

"I'm sure he's looking for things that are a lot more valuable than that," Tank said, his mouth turning down. "Whatever he doesn't find himself, he'd pay plenty to get hold of. You can be sure he didn't dive for that cannon himself."

Skip watched as Buckley and his assistant walked farther down the beach. He looked thoughtful. "Guys like that," he said, "are used to getting whatever they want."

Tank turned to Maryellen. "What did you talk to Buckley about?" he asked sharply.

The question took Maryellen by surprise. "Why, I—I mean, he—asked what you were doing," she stammered. "I just told him Jerry was diving to study fish."

"From now on, just keep away from him," Tank said tersely. "That man's nothing but trouble."

Maryellen nodded, looking down at her sand-covered feet to avoid Tank's gaze. It was almost as if Tank were scolding her for having talked to Mr. Buckley. She couldn't see that she'd done anything wrong at all! At least Mr. Buckley was friendly—and interesting, too. She turned toward Jerry, hoping he might stick up for her, but he said nothing.

"Okay," Maryellen said finally, even though she didn't really feel like anything Tank had said to her was okay at all.

Tank was in a huge hurry now. "Let's shove off," he said, tugging the bow of the boat toward the water. In an instant, Jerry and Skip met at the back of the boat and pushed it the final few feet into the waves.

"Sorry, Ellie," Jerry called back. Then he swung himself into the boat. "We've got a lot to do right now. I'll see you another day, all right?"

"Sure," Maryellen said, doing her best to sound

unruffled by what had just happened. "See you later, alligators!"

Maryellen walked slowly back to the shack, dragging her feet in the warm sand and reflecting on the strange warning she'd just received. What could be so bad about Mr. Buckley, and why on earth should it matter to Tank?

chapter 3

Lost and Found

THE NEXT AFTERNOON, Maryellen biked
to the pier, then took a long walk on the beach to pass
the time until she met her friend Davy Fenstermacher
at the clock tower. She searched the sand for interesting seashells, but all the shells she spotted were
broken. She would have to get to the beach earlier in
the day if she ever wanted to beat the tourists, who
seemed to claim the prettiest and most colorful shells
to take home as souvenirs. As she strolled along,
Maryellen found herself scanning the beach for any
sign of Mr. Buckley and Pete, and listening carefully
for the clicks of their metal detector. She wasn't sure
whether she wanted to see them or not.

By the time Maryellen got back to the pier, she
guessed it was about time to head over to the plaza

to meet up with Davy, who was planning to come straight from a special football practice. She walked her bike up Main Street so she wouldn't have to pedal uphill—with no gearshift, her bike was no match for hills. As she trudged up the street, she couldn't help thinking about the first thing she would buy if she were as rich as Mr. Buckley: a bike with three gears.

At the top of Main Street, Maryellen hopped onto her bike and rode along Ocean Avenue. She turned off the road and coasted onto the park-like plaza, marveling at the beautiful wall that surrounded it. Every student in Florida learned about coquina stone, a special kind of rock that was studded with ancient bits of coral and seashells. The wall, the clock tower, and the outside of the band shell had all been built with it. Maryellen could spend hours counting the different shells that stuck up from the bumpy pinkish walls.

The far end of the plaza was framed by the huge

band shell. Its wide stage and curving roofline were bookended by two tall towers, and a long parapet bridged the towers high across the top. Maryellen always expected a fairy-tale princess to open one of the tower windows and gaze down upon her subjects strolling below.

The afternoon sun was growing warm, so Maryellen parked her bike and plopped down in the sliver of shade cast by the clock tower. At its very top, there were four clock faces, one on each side. Instead of twelve numbers, each clock face had twelve letters. On the upper half, they arched around from the 9 to the 3 position and spelled D-A-Y-T-O-N-A. On the bottom half, they curved upward to spell B-E-A-C-H. The clock was a town landmark; Maryellen's mother often sent her parents a postcard of the clock with a funny note that said, "It's high time you came to Daytona Beach!"

Right now, the big hand on the clock was on the lowest A, and the small hand was at the N, so

Maryellen knew it was almost two-thirty. Davy would be along any minute. She leaned over the fountain that burbled into a pool at the base of the clock tower and splashed her hand into the water. Just then, Davy skidded his bike to a stop in front of her.

"Half past N," Davy said. "I'm right on time— Daytona time, that is." Maryellen laughed. The clock could be a little confusing, but it was lots more fun than a regular clock.

Like Maryellen, Davy was already in his swim-suit. A towel was rolled up behind his bike seat. "Last one in is a rotten egg," he said, pedaling off.

Maryellen was eager to swim, too. Although the December air was cool, she knew she would feel warm enough under the water. She hopped on her bike and quickly caught up with Davy. They coasted down Main Street to the beach, then walked under the pier and chained their bikes together against one of the thick wooden posts that supported it. Just before closing the padlock, Maryellen felt for her key, which she kept strung on an old shoelace. She wore the key like a necklace whenever she rode her bike.

She snapped the lock shut. "Now that I keep my key on the string," she said, "I never lose it. It's a pretty good idea, if I do say so myself." Maryellen was not naturally tidy or organized, so she felt happy whenever she came up with a clever solution.

"You're always coming up with ideas," Davy said, grinning. "I guess sooner or later, some of them *have* to be good!"

Maryellen knew Davy was just kidding. They had been friends almost all their lives, and living right next door to each other meant that Davy had been around for most of Maryellen's Big Ideas—some of which had turned out great and some of which had turned out, well, not so great. It felt nice to know that they were friends either way, and that they liked the same things—or most of them, anyway.

"Are you going to the dance on Saturday night?" Maryellen asked as they carried their beach towels toward a spot near a lifeguard tower.

Davy made a sour face. "I'll go just to watch," he said. "Football's my game—not dancing."

"I want to dance this year, if I can," Maryellen said. "Carolyn has been trying to teach me, but I'm terrible at it. The faster the music plays, the quicker I forget the steps. My feet get all tangled." She pointed toward the end of the wooden pier where a group of brown pelicans were waddling awkwardly, looking for scraps of food dropped by visitors. A few of the birds suddenly took flight, soaring gracefully on currents of air. "See those pelicans? We have a lot in common."

Davy shot Maryellen a puzzled look, which she ignored. "Right now I look pretty clumsy when I dance, like those birds do when they walk, but once I get better, maybe I'll be as graceful as a pelican flying across the sky."

"Sure," Davy said. "You'll be gliding on air."

Maryellen shook her head. "I'll never be that

good," she said firmly. "I just want to be able to dance without tripping over my own feet. Carolyn said she might dance with me for a song or two, but only if I'm a lot better than I am now. She won't want to dance with a pelican, that's for sure."

When they reached the water's edge, Maryellen waved up at the lifeguard, who sat on the tower high above them, dabbing a line of white cream on his nose to block the sun. They dropped their towels on the sand. Maryellen pulled off the old shirt of her father's that she used as a cover-up. Then she and Davy splashed into the waves. Davy dived beneath the surface and came up shaking his head so that his crew cut sent out a wild spray of water. "Race you to the pier," he shouted.

"Go!" Maryellen called. She swam as fast as she could, legs kicking hard. She just barely beat Davy to the pier, but on the way back, her legs were tired and Davy beat her by a body length. Breathless, Maryellen put her arms down in the shallow water, anchoring them in the muddy sand as she kicked against the waves. She scanned the beach again, half hoping she would see Mr. Buckley just so she could point him out to Davy.

"Too bad you weren't with me yesterday," Maryellen said. "I met a man who was hunting for lost treasure on the beach. His name is Atherton Buckley, and he has a special machine that can detect things hidden under the sand."

Davy listened intently as Maryellen explained how the metal detector worked. Ever since he and Maryellen had seen *Treasure Island*, they had both been fascinated by the idea of hidden treasure. "Jim Hawkins would have found the treasure a lot faster with that machine," he speculated. He floated on his stomach like Maryellen, his hands planted in the sand. "Wouldn't it be nifty if they made a movie like that and set it at Daytona Beach? They could use Mr. Buckley's detector in it."

Maryellen thought a movie set in her town

would be pretty boring. A movie needed bad guys,
and Daytona Beach just didn't seem like a place that
would have any. Jerry's boss, Tank, was certainly
unfriendly, and with his head wrapped in a scarf,
he looked a bit like a pirate, but Maryellen couldn't
imagine him as a villain. "The detector would be
cool," she agreed, "but there aren't any pirates around
now to make it interesting."

"No," Davy agreed. "But there are sharks! That
would make the movie really exciting." He opened
his mouth and snapped his teeth together. "Watch
out! I'm a shark!"

Maryellen giggled. "You're not a very vicious-
looking shark," she said, standing up. Water poured
from her bathing suit and dripped into the ocean.

"Well, our football team *is* called The Sharks,"
Davy said, "and I'm plenty tough when we play.
In our last game, I made more tackles than any
other player."

The two friends waded back to shore. The tide

was going out, leaving small furrows of wet sand between shallow pools of water. Maryellen amused herself by jumping from puddle to puddle as if she were Jim Hawkins trying to dodge the sinkholes in the swamp on Treasure Island. Just as she landed in one puddle, she spotted the fluted edges of a scallop shell peeking out. She reached down and picked it up. It was large, and unbroken.

"Aha!" she cried. "I found one the tourists missed!" She rinsed the sand off the shell, revealing reddish coloring along its ridges. "Beverly will love this for her shell collection."

Maryellen held the shell out to Davy, and then bent to look for more. As the sun emerged from behind a small cloud, she spotted another round edge poking up from the wet sand. "This might be another good one," she said, digging under it with her fingers.

What she pulled from the sand didn't look like any shell Maryellen had ever seen. It was white and bumpy like some shells, but perfectly circular, with a hole in the middle. She swished the object through the water to rinse off the sand, then scraped her fingernail over the white crusty spots stuck to it. "I think it's a ring."

"Neato," Davy said, coming over to inspect.

Maryellen tried the ring on her pointer finger, but it was far too large. It even slipped easily off her thumb. "It'll fall off if I wear it," Maryellen said, but the words were only half out before she realized she had the perfect place to put the ring. She untied the shoelace around her neck and slid the end of the lace through the ring. It pinged against the bike key as she retied the lace.

"It's a good thing Mr. Buckley wasn't sweeping his detector through the water," Maryellen said, slipping the shoelace back over her head. "He would have found this first." Then she remembered something. "Mr. Buckley said he turned in the wedding ring he found. I wonder if I should turn this in, too."

"I don't know," Davy said. He toweled off and slipped his T-shirt back on. "That thing looks like it's been buried under the sand for ages. Whoever lost it must be long gone."

Maryellen nodded. The ring did look old, and she thought it would be nice to keep it. She shook out her wet hair and ran her fingers through the tangles. The cool breeze sent goose bumps racing up and down her arms, and she dried off as best she could. She slipped the old shirt over her wet bathing suit, trying to warm up.

"The ring could have been lost by some tourist from—from—Vermont!" she said, trying to imagine a wintry location up north. "Or maybe someone lost it ages ago while they were on a fishing trip. Maybe it took years for it to wash up this close to shore."

"Let's show it to Joan," Davy suggested. "She might have an idea of what you should do with it."

They ambled over to Sandy's Beach Hut. "Shhh," Sandy said as they approached. "It's a slow day for

customers, so I'm letting Joan study." He motioned
to a nearby spot, where Joan sat cross-legged in the
sand, her head bent over a book.

Maryellen didn't want to bother Joan, but she
really did want to ask about what she'd found. She
pulled the ring from under her collar and held it
out to Sandy. "I found this in a sandbar just past the
pier," she said quietly. "Do you think anyone might
still be looking for it?"

Sandy looked closely at the ring. "That looks
positively ancient. Maybe you've found some buried
treasure."

Maryellen pictured a stash of pirate loot and
felt goose bumps on her arms again, but this time
it wasn't because she was cold. She looked at Sandy
doubtfully. "You don't mean pirate treasure, like in
Treasure Island?" Maryellen knew it was crazy even to
imagine that, but it wasn't easy to shake the idea.

"Aaarrr," Sandy growled, rolling his eyes and imi-
tating Long John Silver, the peg-leg pirate character

from the movie. He squinted at the ring, and then scraped at the top with his fingernail. "Lookee here, mateys. Methinks there might be something carved in the top."

Maryellen peered at the ring, but all she saw was the rough white coating that almost completely encrusted it. It looked nothing like the sparkling gold and jewels that young Jim Hawkins found at the end of the movie. "If this is what real treasure looks like, then I don't know why anyone would waste time looking for it," she declared.

"Anyway," Davy said, "who ever heard of pirate treasure buried at Daytona Beach?"

"Not so fast," Sandy said thoughtfully, in his own voice. He sat on the stool he kept behind the stand. "I'm something of a history buff. For years, I've been reading about the French and Spanish rulers who sent explorers to claim new territory around here. Hundreds of years ago, they scouted the seas up and down this coastline. Plenty of ships were lost just offshore." He gestured out toward the horizon. "In fact, there's a plaque up on the plaza to remember an entire fleet of French ships that went down in a storm right off the beach here."

Davy leaned closer and lowered his voice. "Did any of the sailors survive? Or were they eaten by sharks?"

"Nearly all the sailors managed to swim to shore," Sandy said, "which shows you how close they were. Now, I'm not saying this ring is from one of those ships, but who knows what might have been lost in these waters?"

Maryellen looked at the ring with new interest. She arranged the shoelace under the collar of her shirt so the ring was on display. As she and Davy walked back to their bikes, she said, "That's probably just a made-up story." Then she hesitated. "Right? I mean, even if it's true, it doesn't have anything to do with this ring."

"That's the problem with grown-ups," Davy said.

"You can't always tell when they're serious, and when they're just pulling your leg."

"I know," Maryellen agreed. Still, Sandy had sounded convincing.

They walked their bikes toward the large open plaza, where a group of workers were busy setting up for the dance. Some were perched on ladders, adding lights around the opening of the band shell. Others were busy stringing rows of bulbs on the two towers at either side. As Maryellen tried to imagine how bright and festive everything would look when the party began and the plaza was filled with people and music, she heard someone calling her name. She turned toward the street and spotted Carolyn waving as she pedaled toward them on her bike.

"I came to pick up more posters," Carolyn said. She got off her bike, took the last poster from her basket, and unfolded it with a flourish. An illustration of the clock tower, with the band shell behind it, filled the page.

Daytona Beach's Annual Dance
Rock Around the Clock!
Live Band! Free Admission!
7 p.m. Under the Stars

"I just *have* to dance Saturday night," Maryellen exclaimed. But even as she spoke, she felt a flash of doubt. Could she learn the steps in time to be part of it all?

"You can wear your poodle skirt," Carolyn suggested. "It's perfect for twirling!"

"Twirls?" Maryellen asked. "I don't think I'm ready for that yet."

"We'll practice those tomorrow," Carolyn said. "You'll want a few new moves to fit in with all the other dancers." She hopped back onto her bike and pedaled off, her ponytail swinging.

Maryellen's heart raced a bit, just imagining herself twirling in time with the music, her poodle skirt flaring out around her. She didn't know whether she felt excited or just plain nervous. She was glad when Davy shifted the subject back to what Sandy had told them about shipwrecks and the ring.

"Let's go see if there really is a plaque on the wall," he suggested.

They walked along the boardwalk next to the wall that enclosed the plaza. The wall was built with the same rough coquina stone that made the clock tower and the band shell so fascinating. Although Maryellen knew the plaza hadn't been built that long ago, she couldn't help imagining it as an ancient fortress. *The band shell with the two towers on either side could be a castle,* she thought, *and the windows in the towers would be great for a pirate lookout. Now **that** would be perfect for a movie set.*

"Can't you just picture explorers digging up rocks to build all this?" she wondered aloud.

"I sure can," Davy said. "This thick wall is perfect for a fort. Look how tall it is here." He craned his neck, trying to see over the top. Suddenly, a smile spread across his face, and he leaned back against the wall. "Well, I've just answered one little question."

"What's that?" Maryellen asked.

Davy hopped to the side and pointed to a bronze sign attached to the wall high above them. "The plaque!" he exclaimed. He read it aloud:

THE FLEET OF

JEAN RIBAULT

FRENCH ADMIRAL

WAS WRECKED

ON THIS BEACH IN 1565.

"Wow!" said Maryellen. "Sandy wasn't just teasing us. There really were shipwrecks here."

"Maybe that's one more clue about your ring," Davy said. "What if it really *is* lost treasure from some ship? That would make you as lucky as Jim Hawkins."

"And luckier than Mr. Buckley," Maryellen

added. "I'd rather have this ring than a few nickels and dimes."

"You know," Davy said thoughtfully, "I wouldn't mind finding my own treasure. If that ring washed up close to shore, there could be more stuff near where we found it. What do you say we come back here tomorrow and do some digging?"

"That's a great idea," Maryellen agreed. "Let's come really early, before the beach gets crowded." Maryellen knew it was practically impossible that, after hundreds of years, she had found treasure from a shipwreck, but it was almost as exciting to think about as the big dance. And maybe—just maybe—there were other interesting things buried under the sand.

chapter 4

An Unexpected Offer

THE NEXT MORNING, before the sun had risen, Maryellen woke up and felt for the ring under her pillow, where she'd put it before going to sleep. Even if the ring wasn't exactly treasure, it did seem like it had a story to tell—a story she wanted to know. A few dim rays of light were creeping into the bedroom, and the rest of the family was still asleep. Maryellen slipped silently out of bed and closed the bathroom door before turning on the light. She picked at the crust that coated the top of the ring. What did Sandy think he saw there?

Maryellen filled the sink with hot water, swished in a few drops of shampoo, and let the ring soak for a few minutes. With her hands in the soapy water, she tried again to clean the top. A few tiny pieces of crust broke away, but not enough for Maryellen to see any design. *Was* there a design? Was it someone's initial? Or even a name? She scraped with her fingernail until she heard Beverly stirring in her bed. Quickly, she drained the sink and dried the ring. She didn't want to have to share the discovery with her little sister or brothers just yet.

Without making a sound, she dressed in long pants and a T-shirt, and then pulled a sweatshirt over her head. She knew the December morning would be cool. She strung the ring back onto the shoelace along with her bike lock key, and pulled the knotted string over her head. In the kitchen, she buttered a piece of bread and ate it standing up.

As soon as the sun had fully risen, Maryellen slipped out the kitchen door. Inside the garage, she rummaged around for something she and Davy could use to dig through the sand. She found two rusty beach shovels and dropped them into her bike basket. Then she walked across the narrow side yard and rapped her special signal on Davy's window. *Tap, tappety, tap, tap. Tap, tap.* In a flash, Davy poked his head from behind his blue curtains. He soon came outside and retrieved his own bike.

"I could hardly sleep," Davy said. "I'm just itching to see if we can find any more treasures."

If the ring really is treasure to begin with, Maryellen reminded herself.

The beach was nearly deserted, and the ocean was blanketed in fog. It would take time for the sun to burn off the haze. A flock of seagulls huddled together on the sand, the feathers on their heads ruffled. *They must be cold,* Maryellen thought. Still, she was glad that the cool, foggy morning would keep most people away from the beach. She and Davy were free to explore.

They leaned their bikes against the empty lifeguard tower. Maryellen took the two sand shovels from her battered bike basket and handed one to Davy. They pulled off their shoes, rolled up their pants legs, and stepped onto the sand bar that had formed near the shore. The cold, wet sand sent a shiver up Maryellen's legs.

"Let's start digging," she said. "Maybe we'll warm up."

Maryellen tried to pinpoint the place where she'd found the ring by looking at the lifeguard tower and guessing how far she had walked toward the pier the day before. When she reached the spot, she started digging. Just a few moments later, she felt her shovel clink against something hard and metallic.

Maryellen dug deeper in the wet sand. Her face fell when she pulled out an old bottle cap. She tossed it aside.

The sound of a motorboat broke through the silence. Maryellen looked toward the Main Street pier and saw a small boat coming in to shore. It was Skip's dinghy. Remembering that most mornings Skip and Jerry brought in the conchs they caught together, she looked expectantly for Jerry as the dinghy glided closer to the beach. But she saw only Skip. *Why is Skip alone?* Maryellen wondered, disappointed. Didn't the two always dive for conchs as a team? Quickly, she reminded herself that for a busy student like Jerry, Christmas break probably wasn't a vacation. Like Joan, he probably had studying to keep up with, or work to do on the report he was writing for Tank.

Skip hopped out of the boat, pulled two pails from inside the dinghy, and began lugging them slowly up the beach.

"Hi, Skip!" Maryellen called out.

Skip nodded, but just kept walking.

"Those pails must be heavy," Maryellen said to Davy.

"He probably found lots of conchs," Davy guessed. "But he doesn't seem to be heading toward Sandy's. Maybe it's too early for Sandy to be at work."

"Could be," Maryellen agreed. She looked toward the pier, where Skip was just visible through the fog, struggling under the weight of the buckets. Just then, a second man emerged from the fog and jogged toward Skip. The man's dark green work shirt and heavy boots instantly struck Maryellen as familiar.

"Hey, that's Mr. Buckley's assistant, Pete Jones," she told Davy. "What's he doing here?" She watched as the men seemed to exchange a few words, and then Skip turned away abruptly. Pete waited a moment and then began walking back toward Main Street.

Maryellen tried to make sense of what she'd seen. "The other day, Jerry's boss, Tank, warned me to keep away from Mr. Buckley. I suppose that meant to stay away from his assistant, too. So I guess it makes sense that Skip wouldn't want to talk to Pete." She thought for a moment, then added: "I still don't see what's so bad about Mr. Buckley or Pete."

"If Skip brushed him off," Davy said, "then there must be a good reason."

Maryellen was watching Pete disappear into the

fog when a nudge from Davy brought her back to their project. "Let's keep digging for treasure," Davy said. "We need to hunt while the tide is low."

The two split up and searched in several spots. After nearly an hour of digging through the cold mud, Davy let out a groan. "I'm tired of bending over. This is harder than football practice." He looked around. "And all we have to show for our work is a bunch of holes in the sand."

The holes were already starting to collapse, and water had begun to puddle around the pile of junk they had dug up—more bottle caps, some bits of smooth green sea glass, lots of broken shells, and a rusty spoon. "I think we need Mr. Buckley's detector," Maryellen said, glumly surveying the pile. "We're never going to find anything valuable with these little shovels."

She looked up. The fog was dissolving into thin wisps, and if she squinted, she could just make out the hands on the clock tower face. "I promised to meet Carolyn this morning," she said. "If I'm not up on the plaza when she gets there, she won't wait for long." Maryellen worried that Carolyn was tired of trying to teach her to dance. Today she just had to prove that she really could remember the steps. But could she?

"I'll come with you," Davy said. "With no football practice today, there's not much else to do."

As they walked back toward their bikes, Maryellen was surprised to see Pete sweep past them, the metal detector in his hands. "Hey," she exclaimed to Davy. "He's taking the detector over to the sandbar where we were just searching."

"Too bad for him," Davy said. "I don't think there's anything left to find. We dug a lot of holes."

A funny feeling washed over Maryellen. Why would Pete be searching the very spot where she'd found the ring? It almost felt as if he was following them! She shivered, and then pushed the thought from her head. It was one thing for her and Davy to imagine the ring really was treasure, like in the movie they loved. It was quite another to think that other people thought so, too. Anyway, she reminded herself, Pete couldn't possibly know she'd dug up a ring there. Nobody but Davy and Sandy knew she'd even found it.

The sight of the band shell, where workers had begun to assemble decorations for the dance, swept the last bit of worry from Maryellen's head. Large gray fishnets lay in a heap next to colorfully painted buoys. Dozens and dozens of plastic starfish, sea-horses, and tropical fish had been separated into piles ready for hanging.

"Wow!" exclaimed Maryellen. "It's going to look fantastic when it's all decorated."

"I could have guessed that everything would be beachy," Davy said. "Why don't they do something really interesting—like sports banners?"

A giggle came from behind them. "Sports banners?" Carolyn said, smiling. "Then the entire event would be all boys! Who would they dance with?" She set her transistor radio on a wooden sawhorse and turned it on. "I hope you've been practicing, Ellie."

"I've tried," Maryellen answered sheepishly. "Really I have, but it's almost impossible to do it when I'm home. If you'd been with me the other morning, you'd understand. Mikey was throwing a tantrum, and then Tom wanted to dance with me, and so did Beverly. Scooter was howling to beat the band."

Even as she spoke, Maryellen knew that it sounded like she was just making excuses, and that finding the ring had distracted her as much as everything else had. "I know I haven't practiced enough," she admitted, "but I have something else to show you. Davy and I went to the beach yesterday and we found something really—"

"Never mind," Carolyn said with resignation, taking Maryellen's hand in hers. "Let's see what you remember."

As the two started dancing, Maryellen repeated the steps in her head, trying to match her steps with Carolyn's. Maryellen was glad that the song on the radio was "Money Honey." It was just slow enough for her to remember most of what she needed to keep in mind.

"Not too bad," Carolyn said after a few moments. "Let your feet kind of slide a little when you move." She nodded when Maryellen tried it. "Now let's add a new move—a twirl."

Maryellen felt a flutter in her stomach. "A twirl? I'm not ready for new steps. I haven't gotten the old ones right yet."

"Easy-peasy," Carolyn said. "It's all part of the same dance." She demonstrated how Maryellen should make a turn under her partner's arm, while ending with the basic step.

"That looks tricky," Maryellen said, hesitating.

"Come on," Carolyn urged. She took Maryellen's hand again, started the step, and then twisted her hand, prompting Maryellen to turn.

Holding her breath, Maryellen managed to twirl without falling. She faced Carolyn again, her face expectant.

Instead of complimenting her, Carolyn only frowned. "You're on the wrong foot now."

"I know," Maryellen huffed. "I just keep forgetting where I'm supposed to end up."

Carolyn sighed and turned to Davy, who was watching intently. "I'll bet you could pick this up in a jiffy," she said. "Want to try?"

"No thanks," Davy said. "Dancing is for girls."

"That's right," Carolyn said. "It is for girls—and for guys. You'll see. In just a couple of years, you'll love coming to these dances. And believe me, you won't be dancing alone."

Davy sat and watched intently as Carolyn and Maryellen began to dance again, repeating the steps and dizzying turns over and over. When the girls stopped for a breath, a tall man in a trim suit and bow tie approached. He carried a stack of folded posters in his arms.

"Getting ready for the dance?" the man asked. "I like those fancy twirls."

"Hi, Mr. Palmer," Carolyn said. She reached out and took the posters from him. "This is my sister, Maryellen. I'm teaching her to dance." The man smiled broadly and held out his hand. Maryellen shook his hand politely, and introduced Davy.

"Mr. Palmer is in charge of the whole event," said Carolyn. "He's done all the publicity, and hired the band. He's also overseeing the decorations." She tucked the posters into the basket on her bike. "I'm going to bring these to the guest houses along Ocean Avenue. See you later, alligators!"

"I can't wait to see everything decorated," Maryellen said after Carolyn left. "Most of all, I can't believe there are going to be more lights than the ones that were already up for Christmas. It's going to be magical!"

Mr. Palmer smiled. "That's what I'm hoping for," he said. "This dance brings in a lot of tourists, and we want them to leave feeling that they've had an absolutely thrilling time in Daytona Beach. As word spreads, we hope to draw a bigger crowd every year..." His voice trailed off, and he leaned forward abruptly, his gaze fixed on the ring hanging from Maryellen's shoelace. "My goodness, what do you have there?"

Maryellen tugged at the string where the ring hung. "I found it in the sand yesterday at low tide, right by the pier. It's just some junk that washed ashore." Maryellen wanted to sound casual. She knew that even to friendly grown-ups like Mr. Palmer, it might seem silly to imagine that a crusty piece of jewelry could be lost treasure.

Mr. Palmer fiddled with his tie, and then bent closer to look at the ring. "I don't know," he began, seeming to search for the right words. "It might be more... well, special, than you think." He cleared his throat and added, "There's an easy way to find out, though. I own a jewelry store. My jeweler could tell you if it's trash or treasure. He'd be able to figure out how old it is, and what it's made of."

Mr. Palmer pointed to a row of shops on the opposite side of Ocean Avenue. "My store is just across the street. I can take it over to the store for you right now—no charge, of course, seeing as you're the sister of my best helper."

Maryellen considered Mr. Palmer's offer. It was generous, and it made her feel special to be treated so seriously. It made the ring seem more special, too. She wanted to know its real story, but she wasn't sure she wanted to part with it—even to have it examined by an expert.

Maryellen glanced at Davy, who merely shrugged his shoulders in reply.

"I'll think about it," she said finally.

"Why, there's nothing to think about," said Mr. Palmer. His voice sounded kind and reassuring.

"The ring will be in safe hands."

Maryellen looked toward the shop Mr. Palmer had pointed out. From where she stood, she could easily read the lettering on its green awning: *Palm Tree Jewelry and Gifts.* "Could I just take the ring there myself?"

"Well..." Mr. Palmer began. A little wrinkle creased his forehead. "Well, why not?"

"Thanks!" Maryellen said.

As Mr. Palmer strode off, Davy was already heading toward his bike. "What are you waiting for?" he called. "Let's find out about that ring!"

"Let's go, daddy-o!" Maryellen said happily, starting off behind him. What if the jeweler told them the ring *was* treasure? It practically *would* be like a movie. And if there was an exciting story behind the ring, there was no one better to hear it with than Davy.

chapter 5

A Close Call

MARYELLEN AND DAVY pedaled single-file along Ocean Avenue, past a shop selling beach supplies and another displaying seashells, then parked their bikes under the green awning of Mr. Palmer's store. As Maryellen pulled open the door of the shop, she felt her heart start to beat faster. What would they find out about the ring? As they crossed the threshold, a buzzer sounded, startling her.

At first glance, the shop seemed empty, but as she and Davy approached a glass display case filled with expensive watches and jewelry, Maryellen spotted Mr. Palmer standing in a narrow doorway at the back of the store. He was talking softly with a gray-haired man dressed in a dark suit, starched white shirt, and tie. *Wow,* Maryellen thought. *Mr. Palmer got here even before we did.* The two men glanced up briefly, but before Maryellen could even say hello, Mr. Palmer disappeared out the back of the shop.

In an instant, the dapper jeweler approached the counter. "What can I do for you today?" he asked. His eyes traveled to the shoelace around Maryellen's neck, as if he knew exactly why she had come.

Something about the jeweler's expectant look seemed odd to Maryellen. He seemed far too eager, but she pushed the thought aside. She untied the shoelace knot and carefully placed the ring on the top of the glass case, next to a stacked pyramid of round jars containing pink jewelry cleaner. "I found this buried under the sand. Mr. Palmer said you could tell me if it's worth anything. He also thought you might be able to figure out how old it is."

The jeweler swiftly reached for the ring, weighing it in his open hand. He felt in his pocket and with-drew a small, round lens, like a magnifying glass. "Let's see what it looks like through my loupe," he said. He fitted it onto one eye, squinting to hold it in place as he turned the ring between his fingers. "Ah, yes. Yes, I see..."

"What do you see?" Maryellen asked eagerly.

The man didn't reply, but instead set the ring on a wooden work counter behind the display case. He switched on a light that lit the area brightly, and pulled a small velvet-lined tray from beneath the counter. The tray held a row of slim, shiny tools that reminded Maryellen of the tools the dentist used when he cleaned her teeth. The jeweler selected a small tool with a sharp point and used it to scrape gently at the crust that covered the top of the ring. Patiently, he picked at the top of the ring as tiny flecks of grit dropped onto the counter. After a while, he turned back to Maryellen and Davy and used the tool to trace the outline of a pattern the scraping had revealed on the top of the ring. "Do you see this?" he asked.

Maryellen and Davy peered closely at the ring.

Its top was shaped like a hexagon, with a faint design inside it. "I see something," Maryellen said. "I just can't tell what it is."

"Try looking through my loupe," the jeweler offered. He wiped the magnifying glass and handed it to Maryellen.

She placed the lens against her eye and looked again. Suddenly, the design was magnified, as if the ring had swelled in importance. "There's a leaf, or a flower, I think!" She handed the loupe to Davy and held the ring steady as he peered at it.

"I see it, too," Davy said. "Neato!"

The jeweler cleared his throat. "Indeed, you may have found something quite neat," he agreed. "I can't be certain, but the design might be what the French called a *fleur de lis*—meaning 'lily flower.' It is the symbol of French royalty."

"Would that mean that the ring belonged to a king?" Davy asked.

"I couldn't tell you who it belonged to," the

jeweler answered. "If it was lost recently, the owner would surely want it back. Where did you say you found this?"

"Right by the pier. It was just under the sand," Maryellen said, barely able to control the excitement in her voice. Suddenly, it didn't seem quite so silly to think the ring might be a piece of treasure. "Do you think it could be from a sunken ship? We know a whole fleet of French ships went down in a storm just off the coast hundreds of years ago."

"Aren't you clever?" the jeweler said, pressing both hands against the counter. "Of course, such a find would be extremely rare. Do keep in mind that you aren't in an adventure movie. This is real life and it's unlikely that you've found anything of great value. I couldn't possibly tell you how old the ring might be or where it might have come from without a great deal more study. You must leave the ring with me, and I will learn what I can. I must admit, I'm rather curious."

Just then, the door buzzer sounded. A young couple entered the store and approached the counter. "We're here to look at wedding rings," the young man announced. His fiancée smiled sweetly.

"Just over there," the jeweler answered, pointing to a display case on the far wall. "You start looking, and I will be there directly." The couple walked to the opposite side of the store, and Maryellen soon heard the young woman letting out little gasps of delight as she peered into the case.

"Now, then," said the jeweler firmly to Maryellen, "I don't have any more time to look at your beach find today. Leave it with me and I will research it. You can pick it up in a couple of weeks. Just bring this receipt." He hastily scrawled a note on a small card and handed it to Maryellen. Then he took a little velvet bag from the work counter and held it open in front of her.

Maryellen tightened her grip on the ring. Now that the jeweler seemed so interested, it felt even more important than before. She wanted to know its real story more than ever, but two weeks was a long time to wait.

The jeweler glanced at the customers who had recently entered. "Come, come," he insisted, holding the bag a bit closer to Maryellen. "The ring will be safer with me than it would be on that string."

The jeweler was probably right, Maryellen thought. Where else would she be able to get expert information about the ring? Even if the jeweler was being a bit pushy, Mr. Palmer *had* been awfully nice to make this possible...

The jeweler jiggled the bag impatiently. Maryellen took a deep breath, dropped the ring inside, and watched as he swiftly cinched the velvet bag's drawstrings shut and set it on the work counter behind him. She murmured a polite thank you as the man hurried over to his waiting customers.

Clutching the card the jeweler had given her, Maryellen walked out of the shop with Davy. She felt dazed. Everything had happened so fast. As they exited, the door buzzer sounded again, making her jump. This time, it felt like an alarm going off in Maryellen's head. Something about the jeweler's pushiness felt wrong.

Just outside the store, a surge of doubt stopped her in her tracks. "I don't know, Davy. Something isn't right about all of this. Mr. Palmer was very friendly at the band shell, and he was very interested in the ring. But did you notice that, even though we biked right over to the shop, Mr. Palmer beat us here? He was whispering with the jeweler, and he didn't stay when we came into the shop. He didn't even say hello. Then the jeweler practically forced me to leave the ring with him. I didn't have a minute to think."

She lowered her voice to a whisper. "Davy, what if he didn't *want* me to think about it? What if the ring really *is* treasure? What if Mr. Palmer already knew that and told the jeweler to get it from me? I'm not sure I should have trusted either of them."

Davy answered in a whisper, too. "You could be right, Ellie. Mr. Palmer seemed friendly, but maybe it was a trick. You know, in *Treasure Island*, Long John Silver acted like Jim Hawkins's best friend, but he was just using Jim to get his hands on the treasure. Long John Silver turned out to be the worst pirate of the bunch."

Maryellen thought about how sneaky Long John Silver was. With his chatty pet parrot and his near-constant smile, he'd seemed both charming and trustworthy. At least at first. How wrong Jim Hawkins had been to trust him!

"Do you think I'll get the ring back?" Maryellen asked, feeling pained.

Davy frowned. "Maybe not."

Maryellen peered through the window toward the glass counter where they had talked with the jeweler. On the back counter, just opposite the pyramid of jewelry cleaner jars, Maryellen could see the little velvet bag with her ring inside it. She felt something tighten up inside her. "Well, I know one thing for sure. I'm not going to risk making the same mistake as Jim Hawkins. I'm going to get it back now, before it disappears forever."

"Atta girl," Davy said.

Maryellen marched back to the door of the store and tugged it open. As she and Davy stepped up to the display case, the jeweler glanced up from the array of wedding rings he had set out for the young couple. "What is it now?" he asked, annoyed.

"Excuse me," Maryellen said, "but I've changed my mind. I'll just keep the ring."

"Oh?" The jeweler arched an eyebrow. "I'm afraid I'm too busy to deal with this now. You'll have to return another time. I have customers who need my attention." He turned back to the counter and began polishing one of the wedding rings with a cloth.

As Maryellen stood frozen, wondering what to do next, there was a sudden clattering noise, followed by the sound of glass shattering. *Crash!* She turned and saw sudsy pink liquid spreading across the floor tiles behind the display case. A jar of pink jewelry cleaner had fallen to the floor and smashed to pieces.

"Good heavens!" the jeweler cried, rushing to the counter where Davy and Maryellen stood. He bent down and began mopping furiously at the spreading pink puddle with his cloth.

"I'm so sorry," Davy said, stretching all the way across the counter to survey the damage. "I must have bumped it."

The jeweler glowered up at them, his forehead wrinkled into angry creases. Flustered, Maryellen tried to tidy the remaining jars of cleaner on the counter, wondering why Davy wasn't trying to help.

"We'll help you clean—" Maryellen began, but Davy tugged her arm.

"We've got to leave," he said under his breath. "Hurry!"

The jeweler was still crouching behind the counter, dropping broken bits of glass into a wastebasket, as Davy pulled Maryellen out the door.

"That was a disaster!" Maryellen moaned as she unlocked their bikes. "I never should have left the ring with the jeweler. I might never get it back!" She felt tears welling in her eyes.

"Oh, you'll get it back sooner than you think," Davy said, fumbling in his pocket. "Like...now!" He opened his fist and revealed the ring, its small, newly shined spot gleaming in the afternoon sunlight.

Maryellen swiped at her eyes and stared, dumbfounded, at Davy's palm. "How on earth—?"

"I didn't mean to break the jar," Davy said, handing the ring to her. "I just meant to reach over the counter and grab this while the jeweler was so busy with the other customers. But when the jar fell, it was the perfect distraction."

"You're amazing, Davy Fenstermacher," Maryellen said. "And sneaky."

"Well," he reasoned, "it isn't sneaky if you're just getting back your own ring, is it? But let's get out of here—fast, before the jeweler notices that the ring isn't in the bag anymore."

Before hopping on her bike, Maryellen looped the shoelace through the ring and tied it securely around her neck. As she pedaled behind Davy up Ocean Avenue, she felt relieved to feel the weight of the ring against her skin again.

Her sense of relief didn't last long. Maryellen and Davy turned off Ocean Avenue, and then down Halifax Avenue. As they pedaled along the tree-lined street toward their own neighborhood, they passed Mr. Buckley's stately house. Its red tile roof gleamed in the sun, and overhanging tree branches shaded its long driveway. At the center of a formal garden in the front yard sat an ancient black cannon, aimed toward the street as if protecting the house from intruders. Seeing the cannon made Maryellen wonder about all the other treasures Mr. Buckley was supposed to have collected. She pictured a room full of trunks overflowing with gleaming coins and gold jewelry. Something about that made Maryellen feel uneasy.

By the time the friends arrived home and had plopped down on Davy's back steps to catch their breath, Maryellen knew exactly what was bothering her. "Davy," she said, "do you remember the jeweler saying someone would surely want this ring back if they had lost it?"

"Sure," he answered. "If whoever lost it is still around, they'd want it back, especially if it's valuable. But we don't know much more about it than we did before."

"Well, we know that it's old, and the design tells us that it might be French. Even though the jeweler didn't say so, I think that spot he cleaned off showed it was made of real gold." Maryellen took a deep breath. "I hate to say this, but Mr. Buckley is a collector of ship relics, right? What if he's the one who lost it in the sand? That would explain why he was spending so much time searching the beach. It also would explain why Pete was using the metal detector right where we found the ring."

Davy frowned. "They didn't tell you they were looking for a ring, did they?"

"No," Maryellen said, "but maybe he didn't want anyone to know he'd lost it. Then everyone would be looking for it, and someone might try to keep it—just like Mr. Palmer." She took a deep breath, and added, "I think I'm going to have to at least ask Mr. Buckley if he lost anything on the beach. If he says he lost a ring, and can describe it, I'll have to give it back to him." Maryellen felt her heart sink at the idea that she might not get to keep the ring, but it felt worse to think about keeping it if it really belonged to someone else.

"Hold on a minute," Davy said. "Didn't Tank tell you not to talk to him? I thought he said that Mr. Buckley was nothing but trouble."

Maryellen hadn't forgotten Tank's warning. He obviously disliked Mr. Buckley, but he didn't seem to like anyone, really. "Tank is so crabby that I'm not sure I should believe what he says about Mr. Buckley. Why should I listen to Tank if it means that I can't find out who the ring belongs to?"

"Here we are in Jim Hawkins's shoes again," Davy observed. "Who *can* we trust?"

Maryellen wished she knew.

chapter 6

Treasure or Trouble?

ALL NIGHT, MARYELLEN tossed and turned. Strange dreams flickered through her head— fuzzy scenes of Long John Silver limping after her on his peg leg, trying to capture the ring while the parrot on his shoulder squawked over and over, "Mine! Mine!" The moment she woke up in the morning, Maryellen reached under her pillow and was relieved to find that the ring was still just where she'd left it. *I really am letting my imagination run away with me,* she thought, slipping the shoelace and ring over her neck. *Even if this turns out to be from an ancient shipwreck, it wouldn't belong to any pirate.*

At breakfast, Maryellen tried to hear herself think over the noise of Tom's tuneless singing and the sound Mikey's spoon made as he whacked it against the kitchen table. She pushed her scrambled eggs around on her plate, thinking that her head seemed scrambled, too. The ring felt heavy as it dangled around her neck, as if it were weighing her down. Where had the ring come from, and where did it belong?

Maryellen remembered her fourth-grade teacher, Mrs. Humphrey, saying that whenever you felt unsure about what to do, it was usually because you didn't have enough information to make a good decision. What she needed was *information*, and she was determined to get as much as she could. Picking at her eggs, she decided on a plan. The first step would be to go to Jerry. She could trust him to tell her if it was okay to talk to Mr. Buckley about the ring. The next step would be to find out more about ships that wrecked around Daytona and the kinds of things they carried. That could tell her more about where the ring might have come from. School was out, so Maryellen couldn't ask a teacher. The library over on

City Island wasn't very big, but surely it would have what she needed.

Setting down her fork, Maryellen decided to see if Davy could come along. He had been with her when she found the ring, after all. It was a long shot that the ring was actually treasure from a ship, but no matter what she found out, it would be more fun if she and Davy did it together.

Through the open window, Maryellen heard her friend chanting in a husky voice. "Hut! Hut!" She left her eggs cooling on the plate and headed outside. She slipped through the oleander hedge that bordered their yards and sat on Davy's back step. She watched him practice a series of zigzag runs, turning with his arms up at the end of some of the runs, as if he were about to catch a ball. For other plays, he dove to the ground, arms outstretched, as if tackling an opponent ahead of him. He was a fast runner.

"That looks complicated," Maryellen said. "Are you warming up for football practice?"

Davy came and sat next to her, panting a bit. "We don't practice much once the season is over. So when I can, I try to run through the plays the coach taught us. I need to know them cold."

"How can you remember so much footwork?"

Davy shrugged, as if what he had accomplished was easy. "There are dozens of plays we have to memorize, and the coach draws diagrams to show us where we should run depending on who has the ball. Once I look at the diagrams, my feet develop their own brains. I just make them move and they know what to do automatically."

Maryellen nodded absently. It was hard to focus on what Davy was saying about football when there were so many other things on her mind. "Listen," she said, "if you're free this morning, how about coming with me to talk to Jerry? I want to try to catch him when he's alone, delivering conchs at the beach. I'm going to show him the ring and ask him whether he thinks I should talk to Mr. Buckley."

Maryellen filled Davy in on the rest of her plan to research the ring.

"I'm with you all the way," Davy agreed, pulling off his football helmet.

Maryellen smiled. She and Davy were a good team. They separated to tell their mothers where they were headed, then met up at the curb with their bikes. Before long, they had pedaled all the way to the beach and locked their bikes to a post under the Main Street pier.

Maryellen spotted Jerry nearby with Tank and Skip, all standing next to the dinghy. As she and Davy walked closer, she could see Skip unloading some lumpy bundles from the boat. The bundles were tightly wrapped in crisp sailcloth and tied with rope. Jerry was holding the curious map she'd seen before and jabbing at different spots with his finger. He pulled a red pencil from behind his ear and started marking the map. It was as if he were crossing something out. "Small things...here, and here,"

Maryellen heard him say emphatically. "They were there yesterday and gone today."

Tank shook his head, his face dark.

Maryellen stopped in her tracks a short distance from the dinghy. She didn't like the idea of talking to Jerry when grumpy old Tank was there, and seeing how serious the men seemed, she liked the idea even less.

Jerry's and Tank's voices carried on the ocean breeze. "...they're on to us," she heard. Then, "...project...at risk." Finally, "...retrieve the rest quickly." Tank looked directly at Jerry and Skip and added more clearly, "Against my better judgment, I believe we need to get our lovely lady out of there, too."

Jerry seemed to disagree. He rubbed his hands together nervously.

"She'll be a fish out of water," Skip joked.

"It's not safe for her," Jerry stammered. "You know that better than I do. "

Tank's voice rose. "I know the risks, but what choice do we have?"

"We're either saving her or ruining her," Jerry said solemnly. "I'm not sure which."

Maryellen saw the concerned looks on the men's faces. It sounded like someone was in danger. Suddenly her question about the ring didn't seem quite as important.

"Let's go," she said softly to Davy. "I'd better talk to Jerry another time."

She and Davy walked farther up the beach and sat down on the cool sand, which hadn't yet begun to absorb heat from the morning sun. Maryellen knew she shouldn't have listened to the conversation Jerry was having.

"They seemed awfully worried," Maryellen said. "They were talking about a lady, but there's only men on their crew. So who *is* in danger?"

"Didn't you say that Tank's project is counting fish underwater?" Davy asked. "Maybe they could be talking about a female fish."

"It's possible," Maryellen mused, feeling a bit relieved. "Still, they also said something was missing. Fish can swim away, although I don't think you'd say they were 'missing.'"

"Well, we're not making any progress just sitting on the sand here," Davy said. Maryellen stood up. If she couldn't talk to Jerry, she could at least get on with the rest of her plan. "It's a long ride to the library," she said. "Let's get going."

The library was several blocks away, located inside an old building on City Island, right off the river that ran between her neighborhood and the beach. It didn't have many books for children, so Maryellen didn't go there often and wasn't sure what to do once she and Davy walked inside. She stood in front of the wooden card catalogue and scratched her head. The bulky cabinet had dozens of small drawers, each with its own tiny, neat label, and a handle barely big enough for two fingers. She knew that each drawer held hundreds and hundreds of cards, and that each card contained a description of a different book, along with a code for where to find it on the shelves. But how would she find a book that might tell her more about her ring?

"Which drawer should we check first?" she asked Davy. "S for 'shipwrecks'? J for 'jewelry'? Or maybe T for 'treasure'?"

"How about F for 'France'? Or 'fleur de lis'?" Davy suggested.

"I think we'd better ask the librarian," Maryellen said.

A young woman in a red cardigan sweater greeted them cheerfully at the front desk. Maryellen told the librarian that she was looking for a book about shipwrecks near Daytona Beach and the things that might have sunk with the ships.

"Well, then," the librarian said, "you need a

book on underwater archaeology. You're in luck. Daytona Beach happens to have its very own expert on the ships that have been recovered from these waters. In fact, Dr. Theodore Tenker has written a book all about coastal shipwrecks and artifacts. Come with me."

The librarian led Maryellen and Davy back to the card catalogue. With a swift tug, she opened a drawer and flicked expertly through the cards inside. "This one's for reference use only. That means you can't check it out, but you can look at it here in the library for as long as you'd like." The librarian took a scrap of paper from a box on top of the cabinet and wrote a series of numbers and letters on it.

"That's the call number of the book," she said. "You'll find it in the 500s—those shelves are over by the window."

Maryellen took the paper, hurried over to the shelves with Davy, and quickly found the book. *Compendium of Underwater Artifacts*, the spine said.

She set the heavy book on a nearby table and eagerly began scanning the pages.

With each page she turned, Maryellen felt her excitement fade. The pages were gray with tiny text. There were no pictures. She flipped to the table of contents and looked for a chapter title that mentioned jewelry, the fleur de lis symbol, or anything that might connect her ring with an actual shipwreck. Nothing seemed promising.

"This would take forever to read!" Maryellen groaned. "Even then, I'm not sure it can tell me anything I want to know. I'm not getting anywhere today." She slammed the book shut a bit harder than she meant to, and sat staring, frustrated, at the writing on the book's back jacket.

Dr. Theodore Tenker, it read, *is a distinguished Professor of Underwater Archaeology.* From a small rectangular photo just above his name, the book's author stared back at Maryellen. The man in the photo had thick, close-cropped hair. He wore a suit jacket and tie, its knot just visible at his neck.

Something about the man's unsmiling gaze held Maryellen's attention. *Hmmph,* she thought. *If I'd had to write an endless book like this with no pictures, I'd be grumpy, too.* Then Maryellen felt a flicker of recognition. Hadn't she seen that grumpy look before? Didn't she know that man? She *did!*

"Davy," she said, stunned. "I think that's Jerry's boss! He looks younger in this picture. He's not wearing a bandanna, like Tank, and he doesn't have a beard. Still, it really could be him."

"Wait a minute," said Davy, studying the photo and the name under it. "Didn't you say Jerry's boss's name was Tank?"

"Yes," Maryellen said. "That's what everyone calls him. Jerry and Joan never mentioned his full name." She looked at the name on the book again. "Theodore Tenker...couldn't 'Tank' be a nickname? It's possible, isn't it?"

"It is," Davy said slowly, "but this is a book about

shipwrecks, not about fish. Tank's an expert on fish, right?"

"Right," Maryellen said, taking a deep breath. "Or *is* he?"

A long moment passed in which neither friend spoke. Maryellen stared at the book as if she could see straight through it. Her mind began to race. If the man in the picture was who she thought he was, then what he and Jerry and Skip had been doing might not be at *all* what it had seemed. The curious map she'd found so interesting the day she'd met Tank might not be what Jerry had said it was, either.

"Remember the map Jerry was holding today?" Maryellen asked Davy. "It's the same one I saw them with a few days ago. It looked like Jerry was crossing out things he'd marked on there before. But think about it: How do you put fish on a map?"

"I don't know," Davy said. "They don't stay in one place."

"No, they don't," Maryellen agreed, building up

steam. "Now that I think about it, it's strange that they don't want anyone to see the map. The other day, when I tried to look at it, Tank rolled it up in a flash, like it was a big secret. You only keep a map secret if you don't want people to find out what's on it. Like—"

"Like the map in *Treasure Island*!" Davy finished her thought. "But, really, Ellie, how could they have a treasure map? It's not like you can just walk into a store and buy one."

"Of course not!" Maryellen agreed. She was quiet for a moment. "What if instead of trying to follow a map, they're *making* one? What if Tank found something—something important—and Jerry and Skip are helping him mark where he found it?"

"Like a *shipwreck*?! Like in this book?" Davy spoke so loudly that the librarian looked up from her desk and frowned at him pointedly.

"Yes!" Maryellen tried to keep her voice to a whisper. She had to admit that it seemed impossible.

Still, so many nearly impossible things had happened in the past few days. Just finding a ring in the sand was unlikely. It was odd, too, that Mr. Palmer and the jeweler seemed to be trying to take it from her. She fingered the ring around her neck, rubbing at its rough crust, and an even stranger idea popped into her head. She looked over at Davy and saw that his face had lit up, too. "Are you thinking what I'm thinking?"

"Which is...?"

"That if they have found a shipwreck, this ring might be connected to what they're doing. The ring might actually be..."

Maryellen and Davy finished the sentence together: "...treasure!"

As soon as she'd said it, the word *treasure* felt strange in Maryellen's mouth, and a dark thought began to eat away at her excitement. Mr. Palmer had been so interested in her ring. She'd told him and the jeweler exactly where she'd found it. If Mr. Palmer would try to trick her to get his hands on one little ring, what might he do to get at a whole shipwreck?

"Davy," she said, worried, "did you hear Tank mention that someone knew about the project? He said, 'They're on to us,' or something like that. *If* Tank and Jerry and Skip have discovered a ship-wreck, and *if* this ring is somehow connected to Tank's project, seeing the ring could have tipped Mr. Palmer off to it! If all that's true, the entire proj-ect might be in danger—because of me!"

Davy gave a low whistle. "It's a long shot, Ellie, but if you're right about all this, you *do* need to talk to Jerry about that ring—and fast."

"Let's go," Maryellen said. She snatched up the book and replaced it on the shelf. Then she and Davy dashed past the librarian and out into the late-morning sun.

chapter 7

A Mysterious Meeting

AS MARYELLEN AND Davy pedaled down
Main Street, she scanned the water's edge for Skip's
dinghy. It was moored at the buoy, and there was no
sign of the larger dive boat. She guessed the crew
was out on another dive.

"They probably won't be back for a while," she
said to Davy. "Now what?"

"We'll just have to wait for them if you want
to talk to Jerry," Davy said. "In the meantime, we
should keep a close eye on Mr. Palmer. We might
be able to figure out if he knows what Tank and the
crew are up to. Let's head over to the band shell.
I'll bet he's supervising things there today."

"Good idea," Maryellen said.

"I know a way to the back of the plaza," Davy

said. "That way, Mr. Palmer will never see us coming. Follow me."

Maryellen chugged back up Main Street behind Davy, down Ocean Avenue, and then onto a narrow street she had never biked before. It came to a dead end behind the band shell, with the ocean spread out just beyond.

A few cars were parked along the road, and a bright red Cadillac convertible with the top down caught Maryellen's eye. She loved convertibles and liked to picture herself as a teenager riding in one. Just as she was imagining the sun on her face and her hair flying in the breeze, she caught sight of something else: a machine resting on the sparse grass next to the car. It was Mr. Buckley's metal detector!

Maryellen glided to a stop beside Davy. "That's Mr. Buckley's machine," she told him, "so that must be his car. He and Pete are probably around somewhere."

They leaned their bikes against the slim trunk of a small palm tree and moved through the shadows cast by taller trees toward the looming West Tower on the street side of the band shell. Maryellen wasn't surprised when she spotted Pete nearby. Still, she hadn't expected to find him partly hidden behind the wide branches of a flowering bush. He stood as still as a statue, staring intently toward the tower. *What is he looking at?* Maryellen wondered. *And why is he hiding?*

Maryellen and Davy crept forward, step by careful step, trying to see what Pete was watching. With a sudden shock, she realized that Pete was spying on Mr. Palmer—exactly what she and Davy had planned to do! She ducked behind a stack of crates that had been left at the side of the tower, and Davy scrunched down beside her.

Maryellen had a clear view of Mr. Palmer. The shop owner looked over his shoulder before stacking three bundles on the plaza in front of the heavy wooden door to the tower. They were wrapped in sailcloth and tied with rope. She elbowed Davy. "Those are exactly like the ones Skip took out of the dinghy this morning!" she whispered. Had Mr. Palmer taken the bundles that the crew had unloaded?

Mr. Palmer reached deep into the pocket of his suit jacket and withdrew a clattering key chain. He fanned the keys against his hand, selected one, and pushed it into the lock on the tower door. He pulled open the creaking door and used his foot to hold it as he gathered the bulky bundles and quickly slipped inside. The door closed with a heavy thud.

Maryellen stayed hidden, her eyes moving from the thick door to Pete and back again. After a few minutes, the door opened and Mr. Palmer stepped out. Now his arms were empty. What had he done with the bundles?

"Maybe we should march right over and ask him what he's doing," Davy said in a low voice.

"We can't accuse him of stealing," Maryellen said as Mr. Palmer walked around the front of the tower and disappeared from view. "We don't have any proof. Even if we demanded that he tell us what he brought inside, I'm sure he'd make up a story. This just makes it more important for us to find Jerry as soon as he gets back from the dive. We need to tell him what we saw."

Davy gave Maryellen a nudge. "Look," he said, nodding in the direction of the road behind them.

Maryellen turned to see that Pete was now standing at the back of the Cadillac, behind its open trunk. He was talking with someone standing on the street. Although the other man's voice sounded familiar, Maryellen couldn't place it. When the man emerged from behind the trunk, Maryellen looked at him intently. His face was hidden by a floppy fishing hat and dark sunglasses. His faded blue jacket was zipped up to his chin.

The man gestured to the West Tower. "She's

coming tonight," he said. "When she's safely tucked in, I'll leave a note with instructions." He turned to go, pointing to a large planter as he passed it. "Check the geraniums," he said with a chuckle.

"Buckley will be waiting for her," Pete responded. "Don't let us down."

The stranger hurried away. Pete loaded the metal detector into the trunk, slammed it shut, and slowly drove off.

Maryellen leaned back against the crates, wondering about everything they had just seen and what to do next. "I think we were right to worry about Mr. Palmer," she said. "Even Pete seems to think he's up to something. He was spying on Mr. Palmer, just like we were."

"That's true," Davy answered, "but we can't forget that Pete might be a problem himself. At least that's what Tank seems to think."

"Right," Maryellen said, mulling over what she knew of Pete. She'd seen him searching the sand the day before, right where she and Davy had been digging. Now he was hiding behind bushes and having strange conversations with someone who was obviously trying not to be noticed. "I wonder what those two were planning behind the Cadillac. Do you think it had anything to do with what Mr. Palmer is up to?"

"I have no idea," Davy said. "I don't think we're going to figure it out without some help."

"We've got to talk to Jerry," Maryellen said. "I've got to show him the ring, and tell him what we've seen."

"Let's see if he's back yet," Davy said.

They headed toward the beach, and just before reaching the pier, Maryellen heard a motor backfire and then sputter out. She cupped her hand across her forehead to block the glare of the sun and squinted out toward the buoy. "That's the dinghy. They're coming in."

"I think they've got trouble with the motor," Davy said.

Maryellen strained to see. Jerry seemed to be fiddling with the motor and trying to restart it. It kept revving up and then dying out.

"They're at least three football fields away," Davy said. "There's no way Jerry's going to be back on shore any time soon—even if he starts rowing."

Maryellen's mind raced. Who else could help them? "Joan!" she blurted out. "Of course! Joan will know what to do."

They jogged along the beach toward Sandy's stand, zigzagging around people still sprawled on blankets, enjoying the afternoon sunshine. When they arrived, Sandy was busy mashing a bright green paste in a bowl.

"Joan's off passing out samples of my new menu item," Sandy told them. "I think if people get just a taste of what I'm making, they won't be able to resist."

Maryellen eyed the green paste that Sandy was vigorously mashing. It didn't look irresistible to her, and whatever it was, it couldn't be as important right now as the information she and Davy needed to share. "We really need to talk to her right away," Maryellen said. "Where do you think she went?"

Sandy pointed up the beach, away from the pier. "She went thataway, mateys. It might be a while."

Maryellen scanned the crowded beach. How would they ever find Joan in the throng of holiday tourists? "No Jerry and no Joan," she muttered to Davy. "Now what?"

"Well, you could take a break from whatever it is you're doing and try some of this," Sandy said. He spread some of the concoction on two saltine crackers. "This is *guacamole*—a Mexican recipe I learned from a buddy who traveled there. I made it from avocados that grow all around my neighbor-hood. They just fall off the trees when they're ripe. I was stepping around them when a brainstorm hit me: They're Florida fruit, and they're free! Guacamole might be just the bait I need to lure in a crowd."

Maryellen and Davy gingerly picked up the

crackers. "I dare you to go first," Davy said.

"We'll do it together," Maryellen said, not wanting to be rude. "One, two, three!" As she bit into her cracker a smile spread across her face, despite her misgivings. The guacamole was delicious.

"I didn't know something so green could taste so good," Davy said. "How about another cracker?"

Sandy was busy rewriting his chalkboard menu. *Holy Moly, Guacamole!* he wrote. *Florida's Best!* "I'll tell you what," Sandy told them. "If you kids hand out some samples, I'll fix another basket for you to share."

Maryellen hesitated. They should stay there and wait for Joan, she thought. Or go straight to the pier and wait for Jerry. But that taste of salty cracker and creamy spread had reminded her that the ring—and their worries about Mr. Palmer—had kept her and Davy so busy that they hadn't even stopped for lunch. Davy looked as hungry as Maryellen felt.

"It's a deal," she answered. As Sandy scooped the

dip into dishes, she turned to Davy and said, "If we hand out the samples over by the pier, we'll be right near the dinghy the moment Jerry gets to shore."

Sandy handed each of them a red plastic basket that he'd lined with a white napkin. Nestled inside each basket was small dish of guacamole and a pile of crackers. Maryellen and Davy carried the baskets briskly toward the pier, stopping to offer a taste to everyone they passed. People loved the new spread, and she and Davy made sure to point out Sandy's stand. When one basket was empty, they sat in the sand near the pier to share the other. Not long after Maryellen popped the last cracker in her mouth, she heard the dinghy motor over the roar of the waves and looked up to see Jerry guiding the little boat up onto the beach.

By the time they approached, Jerry was already filling a large net bag with flippers and diving masks. He set it on the beach, and then went back for the air tanks.

Skip and Tank had begun to stack other equipment on the sand, but instead of taking it all away, they dragged the boat back into the water. Then, together, the three men lifted a large wrapped bundle from the bottom of the dinghy. It was far larger and looked heavier than the ones Maryellen had noticed before.

"Look, Ellie, they're dipping it into the water," Davy remarked. It seemed that the crew had purposely dunked the mystery bundle beneath the waves and then hauled it up again, their muscles straining with the weight. Salt water poured from the open edges of the sailcloth that shrouded it.

They struggled onto the beach with the heavy load. Maryellen could see that it still wasn't a good time to interrupt, but now she understood that what she had to say was too important to wait. "Jerry," she called out. "We really need to talk to you."

"Listen, kids," Tank said, his face set in the familiar stern frown, "we've got too much work to do right now. There's no time for a break."

"Sorry, Ellie," Jerry said. "We'll catch up later."

Later might be too late, she thought. By the time Jerry was free to talk to her, Mr. Palmer might have taken Tank's bundles anywhere. Maryellen had hoped to talk to Jerry alone, but she couldn't lose this moment. She would have to tell all of them what she feared—and she had to get them to listen *now*.

Maryellen studied Tank's face. He *was* the man who'd written the book about sunken ships—she was sure of it. If the crew was exploring a shipwreck, she reasoned, and if the ring she'd found was con-nected to their project, then the ring itself would surely get their attention. They had probably lost the ring, and they'd be relieved to learn that she'd found it. Maryellen took a deep breath and squared her shoulders. Swiftly, she pulled the ring on its lace from inside her shirt collar and held it up for Jerry to see. "Do you know anything about this?" she asked.

Skip was the first to see what Maryellen was

showing them. He squinted at the ring and his face grew pale.

Jerry followed Skip's stare and nearly lost his grip on the bundle the men were holding. "Ellie," he said hoarsely. "Where did you get that ring?" He seemed to be trying to keep his voice calm, but Maryellen heard an undertone of accusation.

Maryellen let the ring drop back against her throat and looked from Jerry to Skip. "What's the matter? I found it in the sand at low tide."

"That does not belong to you," Tank said, reaching for the ring. "Give it to me."

Maryellen stepped back. Tank was so bossy! She had come trying to help him and Jerry and Skip, and now all he seemed to want to do was take the ring— just like Mr. Palmer!

Suddenly, a gust of wind lifted a loose edge of the wet sailcloth and Maryellen caught a glimpse of carved, weathered wood with a bare trace of yellow paint stained into a crease. *What is that?*

Maryellen wondered. Was it something from the shipwreck, too?

Jerry struggled to tug the sailcloth back into place without losing his grip on the bundle. His voice grew soft. "Listen, Ellie, there's no time to explain things to you right now, but you've got to trust me. You can't wear that ring for another second. It could be dangerous. If you won't give it to Tank, then bring it to Joan and ask her to put it in a safe place."

"We need to talk to you first," Maryellen stammered. "We think someone—"

Jerry interrupted. "No arguments, Ellie. Do it now!"

"Come on, men," Tank said. "We're going to attract attention if we don't get moving." Then all three continued toward the pier, struggling with the weight of the bundle they carried.

...

Maryellen hurried off with Davy, feeling stunned by what had just happened. Once she was sure they were out of sight of Jerry and the other men, she plopped down in the warm sand. "I think that proves our suspicions," she said finally. "They must have brought the ring up from a shipwreck. They've obviously seen it before."

"Maybe they dropped it in the water when they were bringing it back from shore," Davy speculated.

"Did you see how upset they were when they saw it?" Maryellen countered. "Skip looked like he'd seen a ghost, and Tank seemed furious. If they'd lost it, wouldn't they just be happy to see it? It doesn't make sense."

Maryellen thought back over everything that had happened that day, and all that she and Davy had managed to piece together. Everything that had happened in Mr. Palmer's store seemed suspicious. The jeweler definitely would have kept the ring if Davy hadn't found a way to get it back. It must be more valuable than she had ever imagined.

"There's a story behind that ring for sure," Maryellen said. "If only it could talk!"

Davy nodded, his face grim. "I'll bet Mr. Palmer knows plenty. And I'll bet Pete wants to know a lot more, judging from how he was spying on Mr. Palmer."

"We may not know the whole story," Maryellen said, "but the more I think about it, the more that makes sense. Remember, Pete works for Mr. Buckley, and Mr. Buckley is the treasure collector around here. Pete's probably spying for his boss. They're probably *all* after treasure. Maybe that's why my ring is so interesting to them."

Maryellen was beginning to understand why Jerry had demanded that she give the ring to her sister for safekeeping—even if she didn't understand exactly who she was keeping it safe *from*.

She stood abruptly, picking up the empty baskets. "Well, we need to find Joan and tell her about

Mr. Palmer, since Jerry, Tank, and Skip wouldn't listen." As they started walking, Maryellen pondered what to do about the ring. She wasn't at all sure she could bring herself to give it up—not after all she and Davy had gone through to hang onto it.

chapter 8
Finders, Keepers?

WHEN MARYELLEN AND Davy reached Sandy's stand, Joan was busily filling orders for baskets of guacamole dip and drinks. Business had certainly picked up since they had handed out the samples.

"Thanks for spreading the word," Sandy told them as he took their baskets. "Or should I say, thanks for spreading the guacamole." Maryellen could barely manage a smile. Sandy was funny, but she had too many other things on her mind to appreciate his joke.

As soon as Joan had handed her last customer his change, Maryellen pulled her to the side of the shack, held out the ring, and explained in a tumble of words how she had found it. She told Joan everything they had learned about the ring, and about how Jerry, Skip, and Tank had reacted when they saw it. "Jerry told me to bring the ring to you," Maryellen said. "We think we have a pretty good idea where the ring came from, but we don't understand why they want me to hide it."

Joan's eyes widened with understanding. She let out a long sigh. "I guess I'd better fill you in. As much as I can, anyway."

Joan led Maryellen and Davy to a bench where they could talk without being interrupted. "Tell me what you've figured out," she said gently, "so I know where to start."

"Well," Maryellen said, "we think Tank is Professor Theodore Tenker, an expert in shipwrecks."

"We're pretty sure they aren't counting fish!" Davy added.

"You're absolutely right," Joan said. "Tank is an underwater archaeologist, and his research led him to discover an ancient sunken ship not far from

Daytona Beach. Since Skip owns a dive boat, Tank hired him as both navigator and diver. Along with Jerry, they made a good team to study the site."

"We figured they must have found some kind of sunken treasure!" Maryellen said.

"You could call it that," Joan said. "Tank hadn't planned to bring up anything from the wreck. Scientists would rather leave artifacts in place, so they don't get damaged by exposure to the air—and so that other scientists can go back and study the ship-wreck, too. Tank just wanted to create a map detail-ing every object they saw in and around the wreck. By studying the ship's position on the ocean floor and charting where different items had settled into the sand, they could determine where the ship sailed from, what it carried, and how old it is."

"So their map *is* a treasure map!" Maryellen said. "That's why they were hiding it."

"It needed to be kept secret," Joan explained. "If the wrong people knew what Tank had found and where the shipwreck was, they might loot the site. Then Tank and Jerry wouldn't be able to preserve it."

"But we've seen them bringing up bundles of things from their dives," Maryellen said.

"That's because the ship's location has been discovered by looters," Joan explained. "Skip's been trying to guard the site, but someone has still managed to take whatever items were small enough to bring up easily."

Maryellen felt a click of understanding. "Including my ring," she murmured. No wonder the crew had been so shocked when they saw it dangling from Maryellen's neck. Tank had said that "little things" were missing. Someone had taken the ring from the wreck, then dropped it accidentally—and not too long ago. That would explain why the ring was so easy to spot on the sandbar. Maryellen knew treasure didn't just show up on busy beaches.

She untied the shoelace and held the heavy ring

in her hand. "Davy and I think we might know who's looting the shipwreck," she said.

Joan looked at her in surprise.

"It's Mr. Palmer," Maryellen declared. "We were trying to tell Jerry about him."

"Oh, Ellie, where did you get that idea?"

"It's simple." Maryellen told Joan what had happened at the jewelry store, and about the bundles she'd seen Mr. Palmer hiding in the tower. "I don't think Mr. Palmer is as nice as he pretends to be," she concluded. Yet, as soon as she explained her reasoning, Maryellen realized it didn't account for the fact that things had disappeared from the underwater shipwreck. Surely Mr. Palmer wasn't diving down there himself.

Joan smiled and shook her head. "Actually, Mr. Palmer has been helping Tank. The professor gave him those wrapped parcels. When Mr. Palmer noticed the ring around your neck, he must have recognized what it was immediately. I'm sure he was

trying to keep it safe with the rest of the artifacts."
She put her hand on Maryellen's shoulder. "I think
he was trying to keep you safe, too. If the wrong
person saw such a rare item and wanted it badly
enough, you could be in danger."

Maryellen felt a shiver at the back of her neck.
She had worn the ring openly without realizing how
risky that might have been. No wonder Jerry had
ordered her to take it off immediately. Anyone who
would go to the trouble to take things from
the dive site would have no trouble coming after the
ring—and her.

"Why doesn't someone report the looting to
the police?" Davy said in an indignant tone. "They
should be arrested for stealing!"

"I know it's hard to believe, but right now there
aren't any laws against taking things from underwater wrecks," Joan explained. "'Finders, keepers'
is the only rule."

"Whatever Tank and the crew can bring up now

will eventually be part of a museum display, where people can see it and scientists can study it," Joan continued. "But Skip and Jerry had to salvage so much so fast that Tank desperately needed someplace close to the dive site to store it until he finds a secure spot at the university. The tower is close and has lots of empty space. Mr. Palmer arranged for them to use it for a few days."

"Wow," Davy marveled. "It really is just like what happened in *Treasure Island*. When the looters get to the place where the map says the treasure is, it will be long gone! Instead, it will be safe in a totally different hiding place."

"Do you think the tower *is* safe?" Maryellen asked.

"It's all locked up," Joan said. "Mr. Palmer has given keys to Tank and his crew. No else knows the artifacts are there—besides you two."

"And you," Maryellen added.

Joan nodded.

"Wait a minute," Maryellen said, her voice rising. "There's at least one more person who might know— Pete Jones!" She could barely talk fast enough. "We saw him spying on Mr. Palmer at the tower. A few minutes later, Pete was talking with a man I didn't recognize. They were talking about a lady, and a delivery, and about meeting tonight! What if it's *Pete* who's been taking things from the shipwreck, and now he's just waiting for the crew to bring up the rest of it so he can steal that, too?"

"I haven't heard Jerry mention anything about a woman," Joan said reassuringly. "Besides, he and the others will be watching out for problems, and they'll be sure everything is safely locked up tight when they aren't there. I'll warn Jerry as soon as I can, though. He'll be extra careful." She paused before adding, "You should be, too, if you're going to keep wearing that ring."

Maryellen slipped the ring onto her pointer finger and twisted it unhappily. "Didn't you say the rule was 'finders, keepers'?" she asked finally. "Someone took this ring from the shipwreck, and then, *plop!*— it fell in the water. I came along and found it. So it's mine to keep." She looked at Joan. "Right?"

Joan hesitated for a long moment. "I guess that's a decision you'll have to make for yourself."

Maryellen reluctantly slipped the ring from her finger. A lump formed in her throat. A treasure hunter could look for a lifetime and never find a single treasure. If she kept the ring and had it properly cleaned, she would always be able to admire it, hold it in her hands, and know that she had found buried treasure! Still, she knew what she had to do.

She tried to fix the faint outline of the fleur de lis in her head. As much as she wanted to keep the ring, she knew it belonged with all the other things that had rested at the bottom of the sea for centuries. *Really*, she thought, *it shouldn't be owned by anyone. It **does** have stories to tell, and everyone should hear them.*

She held the ring out to Joan. "I'm glad I did find

this tiny treasure, so it can stay with the rest of the artifacts," she said. "It was exciting to have it, even for a little while."

Joan buttoned the ring into her shirt pocket and gave Maryellen a hug. "Tank will be relieved to have at least one of the missing things back." She stood up and turned to go. "I'm going to finish up at the stand before Sandy thinks I've abandoned ship. It's going to be dark soon, and you two need to get home for dinner."

She brightened a bit and added, "Weren't you going to practice dancing with Carolyn tonight? You can leave the worrying to the grown-ups now. The two of you should just have fun planning for the dance. Don't think about anything else. Now scoot!"

Maryellen and Davy retrieved their bikes and began pedaling toward home. Riding up Main Street, Davy shifted into third gear and pulled far ahead of Maryellen. She pumped her legs to catch up as Davy waited at the top of the hill.

As she puffed up the street, Maryellen's thoughts were whirling from everything that had happened in the past few days. First, she had wondered why Tank had been so angry that she'd talked to Mr. Buckley and Pete. Then, she'd suspected Mr. Palmer of wanting to take the ring—and the rest of the sunken treasure. Finally, she understood clearly why Tank had been so grumpy and so wary of Mr. Buckley and his assistant. She hoped that Joan was right, and that the treasure was safe in the tower. Still, there was no way that she could follow Joan's suggestion to relax and think about the big dance. With all that was going on, she wasn't sure she could think about anything else—let alone practice dancing.

The two friends pedaled across the plaza, weaving between clusters of people admiring the decorations around the band shell. Rows of white lights outlined the larger decorations, and strings of blinking lights spiraled around the trunks of the palm trees. The starfish looked as though they were aglow. The stage was set up for the band, with microphones hanging from the rafters and sound speakers aimed at the plaza. Piles of fishnets were draped gracefully along the sides of the stage, with brightly painted buoys placed on top.

Davy glanced up at the letters on the clock. "It's after A-T, and nearly dark. Can you go a little faster?"

Maryellen hadn't realized it was already past six o'clock. She was definitely late for dinner. She worried briefly that her parents would be upset with her. Yet somehow, she didn't want to head home. As she and Davy cruised toward the road behind the West Tower, she reflected on the conversation they had overheard between Pete and the stranger that afternoon. Despite Joan's reassurance, something nagged at her, and when they passed the planters filled with geraniums and trailing ivy, she realized what it was. The note! The mystery man had said he would leave a note in one of the planters.

She slowed to a stop and gazed at the row of planters thoughtfully.

"Don't you think we should at least try to find out what Pete's up to?" she asked Davy. "I want to know who the mystery man is. I think we should just check if he left his message in one of these pots."

"Okay," Davy said, "but let's make it quick. I'm starving!"

The two tucked their bicycles behind the stack of crates, and then began poking through the bright red flowering plants that filled the closest planter. A tangle of vines spilled out of the pot, making it harder to spot a lone piece of paper. Just as Maryellen was finally about to move to the next planter, she heard a car approaching.

"Someone's coming," she said. A large red convertible came into view down the road. "I think it's Mr. Buckley's car." Maryellen tugged Davy toward the crates where they'd stashed their bikes.

From their hiding place, they watched as Pete

emerged from the Cadillac alone and strode directly to the planter nearest the road. He fished around for a moment, plucked a note from the pot, and quickly scanned it as he headed back to his car. Maryellen's heart sank. The note might have told them what the men had planned. Now she and Davy would never know. Just as she was ready to tell Davy they could head home, Pete dropped the crumpled note onto the plaza and climbed into the convertible.

The scrap of paper lifted on the breeze as Pete drove off. Without hesitation, Maryellen chased the note across the plaza, reaching for it each time it swirled in the air and missing as it tumbled farther away. At last, the paper came to rest on the ground. Maryellen stomped her foot over it. "Got it!" she crowed.

Maryellen took the note from under her sneaker and brought it over to where Davy waited. She smoothed it out, read the message, and then shook her head in disappointment. "Phooey! This makes absolutely no sense at all."

She handed the note to Davy and he read it aloud: "ORABA." He looked at Maryellen in confusion.

"Maybe it's in secret code," Maryellen said. She read the note backward. "Ab-ar-o." That didn't help. She tried rearranging the letters in other combinations, none of which made any more sense. Annoyed, Maryellen stuffed the message into her pocket.

"Let's go," Davy pleaded. "My stomach tells me it's way past dinner. Besides, we're not going to figure this out now."

Maryellen stepped away from the crates. "I wish we knew what Pete was planning," she said, looking up at the tower. "I guess we just have to trust that the treasure is safe in there."

"Joan was positive it would be," Davy reminded her.

Maryellen looked toward the tower. She was about to agree with Davy when she noticed that the door at the tower's base was slightly ajar. "It's supposed to be locked," she declared. "We should push it shut."

"Maybe Tank and the crew are still inside," Davy speculated. He pointed to the smattering of cars and trucks still parked along the road near the tower. "One of those might belong to Tank or Skip."

Maryellen considered what Davy had said. Then a more troubling idea came to mind. "What if someone's about to steal everything that's already stored here? Even worse, what if they've already taken it?"

"Maybe we should call the police," Davy said. He fished in his pocket. "I've got a dime for the pay phone."

"They wouldn't be happy with us if it was a false alarm. We don't have any proof of anything," Maryellen said, trying to be practical. "I think we should just peek inside and check to see if the bundles are there. If they are, we'll make sure the door is locked tightly when we leave."

Maryellen couldn't hold back a small smile. "While we're at it, we just might take a quick look at what they've stashed there. Wouldn't you love to see sunken treasure up close?"

She pictured the scene in *Treasure Island* when Jim Hawkins finally came upon the treasure, which had been hidden in a cave on the island. What an amazing moment! As uncertain as she felt about going into the tower, she knew she couldn't pass up the chance to see something so rare in real life.

Davy didn't need any more coaxing. They slipped into the tower, leaving the door just as they had found it. As they entered the shadowy tower, prickles of fear raced up Maryellen's arms. She stood close to Davy until her eyes adjusted to the dusky light.

Maryellen looked around the narrow entry. There was a closed door just to the right, and a steep, winding staircase stretched up ahead of her. She tried the door, which opened to a small room filled with electrical wires and equipment. Maryellen closed it quietly.

"The treasure must be stashed someplace else," she said, peering up the dim staircase. "I hope it's up there, and that no one has beaten us to it."

"There's only one way to find out," Davy said with determination. They both took a deep breath and began to climb.

chapter 9

Casting a Wide Net

ROUGH WALLS LINED the cement stairway inside the tower. Maryellen climbed silently next to Davy, wondering if they were making a mistake by continuing on. After each step, Maryellen stopped and listened for voices or footsteps. What would they do if they caught the thieves red-handed? Could she and Davy escape?

A small window at the top of the stairs cast a dim light down a narrow, curved hallway lined with closed doors. Blinking lights from the decorations outside sent shadows dancing across the floor and walls. Davy and Maryellen began cautiously testing the doorknobs along the hallway. The first few were locked tight.

"If the treasure's in one of these rooms, we'll

never know," Maryellen said, discouraged. Davy had already skipped ahead a few doors to one that remained open a crack, allowing a pale sliver of light to escape into the hallway.

"Over here!" Davy whispered, motioning to Maryellen. He pushed the door open and they slipped into the room.

Maryellen stopped, stunned. In the glimmer of the plaza lights that filtered through the small windows, she saw piles of sailcloth-shrouded bundles glowing like tired ghosts. "The treasure's here!"

As she and Davy crept between piles of salvaged objects, Maryellen knew they should move quickly. Still, it was hard not to linger. Peeking carefully under cloths and into bags, they saw corroded tools, dented armor, and cracked pottery. Beneath one cloth lay a heap of metal plates coated in a moldy-looking green crust. Under another, to Maryellen's astonishment, lay a jumbled mass of tarnished metal swords. Davy ran his hand over the barnacle-encrusted hilt of one of them. He tried to pull one of the swords from the pile, but even with two hands he could barely lift it.

Maryellen tried to picture the burly men who had sailed across the ocean hundreds of years ago. They had eaten from those plates and brandished those swords in battle, she marveled. The room held no trunks of sparkling jewels or coins. In fact, nothing looked remotely like the scenes in *Treasure Island*, but somehow that only made it more fascinating—and a bit spookier.

"Where's that big heavy bundle that the crew was carrying on the beach this afternoon?" she whispered. She scanned the piles until her eyes fell upon a long, thick item set apart from the others. A rivulet of water had formed under it, reminding Maryellen of the heavy bundle Tank and his team had dunked in the water earlier that day. She knelt down and pulled open a loose corner of the sailcloth. As Davy looked over her shoulder, she gently removed a layer of wet rags that hid the item from view.

"Oh!" Maryellen gasped, her heart thudding. "She's beautiful!" They stared at the carved wooden face and torso of a woman. On the carving's badly eroded surface, Maryellen could make out the barest outlines of flowing curls and a billowing dress. A pale trace of yellow clung to the waves of her hair, and a hint of blue showed on the bodice of her gown. Maryellen guessed that the figure had decorated the bow of the ship. She tilted her head up and leaned forward as if she were a figurehead pushing into the wind.

Suddenly, Davy put a warning finger to his lips. Heavy footsteps were thudding up the staircase. He and Maryellen quickly replaced the wet rags on the figurehead and tugged the sailcloth back into place. They glanced around the room, frantically looking for a place to hide.

Davy grabbed Maryellen's arm and pulled her behind a large broken chair in a dark corner of the room. Together, they huddled behind it as the door squeaked open and footsteps grew closer.

Someone had entered the room, but Maryellen didn't dare peek out from behind the chair to look. *Who could it be?* she wondered. Jerry? Or Skip or Tank? If so, she and Davy didn't need to hide. But what if it was someone else—like Pete? Maryellen knew they couldn't take a chance. She held her breath and waited as the soft noise of trickling water punctuated the silence. Maryellen watched the floor with concern as a puddle of water inched toward her feet. If the person tried to mop it up, he would surely discover their hiding place.

Maryellen held as still as the wooden figurehead. She heard the sound of metal against the floor and a faint sloshing. Whoever was there must have set down a bucket. Would he or she be back?

When Maryellen finally heard the door close, she let out a ragged breath. She and Davy stayed motionless until they heard the thud of the tower door below. Silence enveloped the room. They emerged from behind the chair and tiptoed to the window. Stretching as tall as she could to peer over the sill, Maryellen watched the street below. After a few moments, she saw a figure cross the scraggly grass and open the door of a dark pickup truck parked on the street opposite the tower. Maryellen squinted at the man, studying his gait and his size. "It was only Tank," she said at last. "He must have left the tower door unlocked while he filled a bucket with seawater. I'll bet he was just on the beach when we came inside."

Davy watched the man climb into the truck. "I think so, too," he agreed. He stepped around the bucket Tank had left next to the figurehead. "He sure seems determined to keep this thing wet. I wonder why."

"Me, too," Maryellen said softly. "We can ask him that later. Let's get out of here."

They closed the door behind them and started

down the stairway, running their hands along the rough cement wall for balance. At the landing, they paused and looked out. To Maryellen's relief, the band shell was deserted. No one would see them leave. They had continued barely a few steps when Maryellen stopped in alarm. She heard the heavy door to the tower creak open, followed by the sound of light footsteps on the stairs.

"Someone's coming!" she whispered. "It can't be Tank. We just saw him leave." They raced back up to the second floor hallway. Maryellen thought fast. If it was the thief, the treasure room was the last place they should try to hide. But where could they go?

As the footsteps below drew closer, she spied a metal ladder leading to a square opening in the ceiling above them. It must be a way to climb higher up into the tower. She pointed to the ladder and began climbing. Each rung was spaced so far from the rung below it that her legs were barely long enough. She held tightly to the sides, trying not to fall.

The footsteps came closer. "Hurry up!" Davy hissed, giving Maryellen a push. She scrambled as fast as she could onto the floor above. An instant later, Davy pulled himself up from the last rung. They flattened themselves against the floor and peered down through the opening.

A shadowy figure came into view at the top of the stairs. Even in the semi-darkness, the man's blond hair was unmistakable. It was Skip! Just as Maryellen was about to call out to him in relief, a sinking feeling washed over her. The blue jacket Skip was wearing looked a lot like the one worn by the man Pete had been talking with that afternoon behind Mr. Buckley's Cadillac. There had been something familiar about the man's voice. Had Pete been talking with *Skip*?

Unsettled, Maryellen recalled the foggy morning she and Davy had spent digging on the beach. Pete had approached Skip that morning, and Skip had brushed him off as if he didn't know him—and didn't want to. Was it possible that the two men *did* know each other? If so, did that mean she and Davy didn't need to worry about Pete? Or…did it mean that they *did* need to worry about Skip?

Maryellen tried to dismiss her fears as Skip disappeared into the treasure room. Surely it hadn't been Skip talking with Pete earlier. Skip was Jerry's friend, after all. They worked together diving for conchs. Both Jerry and Tank had trusted Skip to guard the wreck. Now he was probably just guarding the treasure in the tower. Yet some small part of Maryellen seemed to warn her to stay hidden. At the very least, it would be embarrassing to have to explain to Skip why she and Davy were cowering in the attic of the tower.

"C'mon," she whispered. "Let's just go before he sees us." She swung her legs over the edge of the opening and scurried down the ladder with Davy just above her. At the bottom rung, she jumped silently onto the floor, and she and Davy dashed down the stairs, trying not to lose their footing.

Davy opened the tower door cautiously, making sure no one else was around before he and Maryellen stepped out. Once outside, they slipped around the side of the building to catch their breath.

Maryellen told Davy what she'd been thinking about Skip. "Do you think we should wait around and see what he's up to?" she asked. "It might be a little silly to worry, but—"

"You're right," Davy answered, not missing a beat. "It *is* a little silly. We thought Mr. Palmer was up to no good, and we were wrong. Skip's not here to steal any treasure. He's working *with* Jerry."

Maryellen let out a long breath. It was true she'd let her imagination run away with her where Mr. Palmer was concerned. Pete might be the person behind the thefts at the shipwreck, but there was little reason to think Skip was involved with him.

"That settles it," Maryellen said, feeling cheered by Davy's certainty. "I'm officially calling it quits.

Let's get home before our parents are furious."

As the two walked toward the crates where they had hidden their bikes, Davy glanced at the lighted clock tower and groaned. "Yikes! It's already quarter past B. We're going to be in a heap of trouble, Ellie. We've got to head home pronto."

"Which way is fastest?" Maryellen asked. "Remember, my bike's not good on the hills."

"Let's take Ora Street," Davy said decisively. "We'll be home in no time."

"Wait a minute." Maryellen tried to keep her voice low. "Did you say Ora?"

Davy nodded.

Maryellen checked the clock tower. "And it's nearly B-A." She froze. Why hadn't she thought of it before? "That's it, Davy! That's the secret message!"

She pulled the note from her pocket and held it out. In the glow cast by the strings of lights on the band shell, Davy read the cryptic message again:

"ORABA." He frowned. "I still don't get it."

"Think about it for a second," Maryellen said. "The first three letters mean Ora Street—O-R-A That's exactly where Pete met with the stranger behind the Cadillac this afternoon. Then the note says B-A. The B is for the small hand on the clock, which is the 8, and the A is for the big hand, which is the 6. Pete was telling the man to meet him on Ora Street at eight-thirty tonight! Something's going to happen here, and soon."

Maryellen's thoughts bounced to Skip, who was now alone in the tower. "Davy," she said. "What if it's not a coincidence that Skip showed up at the tower just before the time Pete wrote on the note? What if he's *not* here to protect the artifacts? He might really have been the man at the Cadillac, and have made some kind of plan with Pete. Don't tell me I'm imagining things now."

"I won't," Davy said solemnly. "I'd say there's at least a chance you're right."

"We have to stay and find out," Maryellen decided. "Are you with me?"

Davy was silent for a moment. "I guess we can't be in any more trouble with our parents than we already are."

They crouched behind the stacked crates and waited silently without taking their eyes from the tower door. A stiff breeze blew in off the ocean and the night air had grown cool. Maryellen shivered in her shorts and thin shirt. Every so often, she leaned out from their hiding place and looked up at the clock tower.

"B-C," she reported. "Eight twenty-five."

Several minutes later, the bright beam of head-lights swept across the plaza, then abruptly went dark. A car crept up to the curb on Ora Street and its engine cut off. Maryellen and Davy turned to see who had driven up. "It's Mr. Buckley's Caddy," Davy said softly.

The car door opened and Pete stepped out. As

silently as a shark prowling the ocean, he moved through the darkness behind the band shell, staring intently at the tower. The seconds ticked by so slowly that Maryellen felt as if she couldn't hold still for another moment. Yet even the slightest movement might give away their hiding place. Goose bumps spread along her bare arms and legs, more from fear of what was about to happen than from the cold ocean breeze.

Finally, the tower door opened and Skip emerged. At first, Maryellen thought he was carrying someone. He bent forward with the weight and grunted slightly as he nudged the heavy door shut. Pete stepped from the shadows, startling him.

"You're late," Skip hissed.

"Quit complaining and get moving," Pete said. Skip leaned to the side and let the heavy load slide from his arms, gently easing it to the ground. As soon as the bundle was resting safely on the plaza, he pressed his hands against his knees, breathing heavily.

"We've got to stow her in the trunk before anyone sees us," Pete said. "There must be ten thousand
lights on this band shell, for crying out loud."

Skip straightened up. "She's not going anywhere
until I get paid," he declared. "We had a deal."

"Old Man Buckley isn't going to pay you a nickel
until she's sitting in his parlor gazing out at the wild
blue ocean," Pete said.

So this is the lady Tank was talking about, Maryellen
realized. *It's not a fish, and it's not a person—it's the
figurehead! Skip betrayed Tank and Jerry so he could sell
the carving to Mr. Buckley, and Pete is handling the deal.*

Skip stepped in front of the wrapped figurehead,
shielding it from Pete. "No money, no lady," he insisted.
"She's coming for a little boat ride with me. You head
over to Buckley's and get my dough. I'll motor over
there and tie up at his dock in about a half hour. When
I get paid, Buckley gets her, and not before. I'd rather
throw her back into the ocean than trust either of you
to come up with the money later." He bent down and,

with a grunt, lifted the wrapped bundle.

"Fine," Pete said, but he didn't sound as though he thought anything was fine. "I'll help you carry her to the boat. The last thing we need is to drop her on the cement. Then we're all goners. I'll have Buckley's payment ready by the time you get to the dock."

Each man took one end of the figurehead. Together, they stepped into the darkness behind the band shell, and began walking toward the ocean.

"I thought I heard a boat motor when we were up in the tower," Maryellen whispered. "Skip must have come in the dinghy. They must be planning to deliver the figurehead to the dock at Mr. Buckley's mansion. If we don't stop them now, they're going to get away with this!"

Maryellen was frozen with panic, remembering what Joan had said about the unspoken rule of "finders, keepers." In just a few minutes, the sculpted figurehead might be lost. Would Tank ever be able to prove it had been his?

"If only we had some help," Davy said. "I should have called the police when I had the chance." Maryellen knew Davy was right. How could they stop two men from stealing such a heavy object? They couldn't just grab it and run. They needed a plan, and fast.

She and Davy crept from their hiding place and followed Skip and Pete into the night. Darkness enveloped the men as soon as they reached the beach, and Maryellen lost track of their position for a few moments until a beam of light flashed not far away. Skip held a flashlight under his arm now, and it cast a dull, wavering light across the sand as the men began moving again.

They lumbered awkwardly under the weight of the figurehead, pausing every so often to catch their breath and adjust their load. They weren't moving very fast, Maryellen thought. Davy was a fast runner—and hadn't he said just the other morning how good he was at tackling? *Davy doesn't brag,* she told herself. *I'll bet he can take them down. I just need a way to keep them from getting back up again.* She thought fast, and a wild plan popped into her head.

"I have an idea," she said, trying to sound confident. "Wait here. Don't take your eyes off those two."

Maryellen darted back to the band shell. Behind her, she heard a heavy truck rattling up Ora Street. She hoped that Pete didn't have more men coming to help, but there was no time to waste checking. She pulled a thick mesh fishnet from a pile at the edge of the stage and tried to hoist it up. Maryellen's arms felt as if they were being pulled from her shoulders. The net weighed more than she expected, and it took every ounce of her strength to drag it to where Davy was waiting.

Maryellen gripped Davy's arm. "It's now or never," she whispered. "Pretend this is a championship football game and you've got to keep those guys from scoring a touchdown."

"I can't tackle two of them," Davy protested.

"I don't even think I can take down one."

"You're good," Maryellen reminded her friend. "In fact, you're great. When I give you the signal, just go for one of them, and give it all you've got. I'll back you up."

Maryellen waited until the beam from Skip's flashlight stopped moving again. "Hut-hut!" she said. "Go get 'em!" Davy took off running and nearly flew through the air as he tackled Skip around the legs. The precious figurehead dropped onto the sand and Skip went down. *Thunk!* His head hit against the carving as he fell.

"Get up! Quick!" Pete yelled, but Skip lay motionless, the wind knocked out of him.

Before he could even lift his head, Maryellen pulled the net over Skip and the stolen figurehead just as Davy rolled out of the way. Pete zigzagged back onto the boardwalk, deserting Skip, who was struggling to lift the netting.

"Pete's getting away," Davy cried.

"Let him go," Maryellen said. "He won't get far. This is the more important catch." They each plopped onto one edge of the fishnet, keeping Skip trapped. "At least we saved the figurehead."

Skip continued to fight against the net. In the distance, Maryellen saw arcs of red lights flashing against the night sky. The lights grew brighter and brighter until they stopped. Car doors slammed, followed by loud voices and the urgent shouts of people running toward them over the sand.

Maryellen looked up and was relieved to see Jerry and Tank standing over her.

"Skip!?" Jerry exclaimed in disbelief. "You're the thief? I trusted you. We were partners."

Skip had stopped struggling inside the net. "You know Tank wasn't paying us half what we're worth," he growled.

Jerry's shoulders slumped with disappointment. He stood at the edge of the net next to Maryellen and waited as a pair of policemen rushed onto the beach, handcuffs at the ready. After the police had taken hold of Skip, Jerry turned to Maryellen and put his jacket around her shoulders. Maryellen had forgotten how cold she was. The jacket felt like a warm hug.

"You must be freezing," Jerry said. "You both must know your families have been frantic. When I learned you hadn't made it home, I called the police and told them about the artifacts in the tower, and the fact that you were missing. I was afraid there was a connection, and I was right."

"How did you ever manage to stop them from taking the figurehead?" Tank asked.

Maryellen turned to Davy. "I had a champion tackler," she said with a grin, "and a fishnet big enough to trap a shark!"

chapter 10
Taking a New Step

MARYELLEN HAD SLEPT late on Saturday morning, tired out from all the excitement of the night before. She'd stayed up much later than usual talking with her worried parents about all that had happened. Now, sitting on a blanket beside Sandy's food stand, she felt the afternoon sun lulling her to sleep again. She fought to stay awake.

"You kids turned out to be pretty good sleuths," Sandy said, giving Maryellen and Davy each a friendly slap on the back. Maryellen perked up, feeling proud of how she and Davy had saved the figurehead. Joan beamed at her.

Jerry and Tank joined them, sitting on two upturned metal pails. Sandy handed out red plastic baskets filled with a hot dog and a side order of guacamole and crackers. Joan passed out cold bottles of soda.

"It's all on the house," Sandy said. He turned to Maryellen and Davy. "We've got to celebrate. You two probably prevented an entire shipwreck from ending up in Old Man Buckley's trophy room. You followed the clues better than any treasure hunters."

"Well, I definitely missed any clue that you were planning to add hot dogs to the menu," Maryellen teased. "I've been trying to get you to do that forever. What made you change your mind?"

"Nearly everyone who walked up to the counter asked for a hot dog," Sandy explained, shrugging in exasperation. "I just had to give in. With so many people coming for the big dance tonight, I plan to stay open late and serve all the hot dogs I can grill."

"This should really be my treat," Tank said. He looked over at Maryellen and Davy. "I know I kept chasing you off, but now I realize that our entire project could have been ruined if you hadn't stuck around." He took in a deep breath and added kindly, "I can't thank you enough for all you did last night. If Pete and Skip had gotten away with that beautiful lady, it would have been a huge loss. Very few figure-heads are found intact, so she's a real treasure."

"But only if she's dripping wet?" Maryellen asked. "I never could figure out why you kept dousing her with seawater."

"That's one of the things archaeologists have learned about preserving underwater wooden artifacts," Tank explained. "The figurehead was still in one piece mostly because it had been buried on the ocean floor. It absorbed the salt water and stayed protected. If it dried out quickly in the air, it would just crumble into bits. We have to dry it out very slowly so that it will last another few hun-dred years."

"I wonder why the ring didn't need to be kept in water," Maryellen mused. "Is that because the salt water was ruining it, instead of saving it?"

"You're pretty much right about that," Tank said. "Metal, even gold, eventually gets eaten away by the salt. That ring was probably protected by the barnacles and crust that had encased it." He turned to Jerry and smiled. "I think there might be another budding oceanographer in your family."

Maryellen thought about that for a moment. Studying the bottom of the ocean would be an exciting life. She imagined herself diving beneath the waves, breathing with an air tank. She would be a modern mermaid!

"As for that ring," Jerry said, "when I saw it hanging from Ellie's neck, I was sure that whoever was raiding our site would do anything to snatch it away—even if it meant putting Maryellen in danger." He squeezed her hand. "I'm just glad that you're safe."

"I'm embarrassed to say I had a slightly more selfish thought," Tank admitted. "I was sure that every treasure hunter from here to Georgia was

going to descend on our shipwreck. You were
a walking advertisement for buried treasure,
young lady."

"You must be really disappointed that Skip let
you down," Davy said to Tank and Jerry. "This
whole shipwreck adventure has felt a bit like being
in *Treasure Island.* Skip turned out to be another Long
John Silver. Jim Hawkins thought the pirate was his
friend, and he trusted him, but in the end, Long John
Silver betrayed him for the treasure."

"Skip betrayed us for a few extra dollars," Jerry
said, shaking his head in disbelief. "I absolutely
never suspected him. We were great dive partners,
and I trusted him completely. He even stood watch
over the site. At least that's what I thought he was
doing."

"Unfortunately, when he was supposed to be
guarding the site from looters, he was really diving
to take whatever he could," Tank said. "He risked
his life diving alone just to bring up as much as he

could sell. By the time you figured out what he was up to, he'd already sold a number of smaller things to Pete."

Maryellen realized that Skip must have been meeting with Pete for days, and that when she and Davy had seen Skip on the beach, the pails he was carrying must have been filled with salvaged items. "Remember that foggy morning on the beach?" she said to Davy. "We thought Skip was trying to avoid Pete, but instead they must have arranged that meeting to hand off pieces of loot."

"Right," said Davy. "Then we saw Pete sweeping the sandbar with the metal detector. Skip must have realized that he'd dropped the ring there the day before, so he sent Pete to search for it with the metal detector."

"Ha!" Maryellen said. "He didn't know I'd already found it until yesterday afternoon. He looked like he was going to faint when he saw it around my neck!"

"He'd love to have sold that ring along with

everything else," Tank said.

"Will you be able to get anything else back?" Joan asked.

"I think we will," Tank said. "I met with Mr. Buckley this morning, and he claimed that Pete had fooled him as well. Buckley insisted that he believed Pete was helping him buy items that Skip had found on his own."

"I don't believe him at all," Maryellen said. "When I met Mr. Buckley on the beach, he was awfully interested in what you were doing out on the ocean every day. I'm sure he connected the items Pete sold to him with your project!"

"I'm willing to let all that go," Tank said, "provided that everything is returned. We have quite a list."

"What's going to happen to Pete and Skip?" Davy asked.

"Probably not much," Jerry said. He shook his head. "Believe it or not, there's not really a law against taking things from shipwrecks. Although there should be." He turned to Maryellen. "Thanks for turning in the ring you found. I know that must have been a tough decision to make."

"Once the artifacts are put on display in our new museum space," Tank said, "I'm going to credit you with finding it. There will be a placard right next to the ring saying, *Salvaged by Maryellen Larkin, December 1955.*"

Maryellen felt a bubble of excitement rise in her chest. She couldn't believe her name was going to be in a museum exhibit. She'd be able to go and look at the ring any time she wanted. It would always be exactly where it belonged—with the rest of the artifacts. Anyone who wanted to would know its story. And she, Maryellen Larkin, would always be part of that story.

Maryellen noticed that the beach was rapidly filling with tourists. Tonight was the big dance, and it looked as though lots of people would be coming.

But she wasn't ready at all. She wondered if it was even worth going.

"With everything that's happened, I haven't practiced the dance steps for days," she told Davy. "Carolyn won't dance with me if it means messing up in front of the whole crowd. Unless we can practice this afternoon—a lot—I'll probably just be watching. Again."

As Maryellen looked longingly toward the band shell, she absently picked up her hot dog from her basket and took a bite. She paused. It tasted different—and delicious. She looked down and saw that some of the guacamole in her basket had dropped onto her hot dog. Was that what made it taste so good? She scooped up even more guacamole with her hot dog and took a bigger bite.

"Hot diggity dog!" she exclaimed. "Sandy, this is the best hot dog ever!" She pointed to the dip. "With your guacamole on top, it's amazing."

Sandy and the others slathered the dip onto their

hot dogs. "I think you're right," he declared, after taking a bite. "It makes my hot dogs unique."

"That's Ellie for you," Davy said. "She's the girl with the Big Ideas!"

Sandy walked over to his menu board. Just beneath the words *Holy Moly, Guacamole!,* he wrote *Exclusive Daytona Dogs!* "No one else on the entire beach has them. They're going to bring in tons of new customers."

"I think it'll be the coolest food around," Maryellen agreed, standing up and putting her empty basket on the counter. To Davy, she said, "Now I'm going to try to find Carolyn. I hope she'll practice with me. Want to come?"

They hustled over to the band shell, where they found Carolyn balanced at the top of a ladder, attaching buoys to a fishnet. "Any chance we could practice before the dance tonight?" Maryellen asked her.

"I'm way too busy right now, Ellie," Carolyn

answered. "I'll help you fix your hair tonight, though." She turned back to her work, chatting and laughing with the other teens who were adding the final touches to the decorations.

Maryellen felt a big empty space open up in her chest. Without help, she'd never be able to get all the steps straight in one afternoon. "Maybe I'll just stay home," she told Davy. She paused. Then she blurted out, "Unless you could help me."

Davy looked blank.

Awkwardly, Maryellen went on. "I was think- ing that you learned your football plays really fast. It's not that much different from dancing, really. Maybe—maybe you could dance with me, just so I could practice the steps."

"Are you kidding?" Davy asked. "If Wayne ever found out, he'd tease me forever!"

Maryellen's face went hot. Davy's friend Wayne the Pain was the last person she wanted to think about now.

Davy tried to explain. "Look, Ellie, it doesn't have anything to do with you. It's just that dancing is your thing, and football is mine. I mean, would you play football with me?"

Maryellen felt a lump in her throat. It was hard to argue with what Davy was saying. She didn't want to play football. She didn't want to dance with Davy, either—or any other boy. She just wanted to be part of the fun.

"Still, maybe I can help you," Davy said. He dashed to the stage and swiped a poster from a pile of leftovers. Then he found a thick pencil that one of the workmen had left behind. He plopped down on the plaza and spread the poster open, picture side down.

With his hand poised over the large blank page, Davy looked up at Maryellen. "Remember when you said that football plays were like dance steps? Maybe they are, but football players learn them differently. We learn them on charts. I'm going to draw

the dance steps for you just like the coach draws
new plays."

Maryellen watched intently as Davy started
sketching.

Maryellen and Carolyn arrived at the band shell
just before seven that night. Maryellen felt almost
like a teen—*almost*—in her poodle skirt and the high,
curled ponytail Carolyn had helped her arrange.
She stood proudly beside her sister, who had wound
her own hair into a French twist so perfect that
Maryellen couldn't see a single one of the bobby
pins she had pushed in to hold it in place. The plaza
sparkled with lights. Reedy notes from a saxophone,
rhythmic drumbeats, and guitar riffs floated through
the air as the band tuned up. An assistant adjusted
the sound system, talking into the microphone.
"Testing, testing, one, two, three." His voice crackled
through the night.

Maryellen was so excited that she twirled on one foot like a ballerina. Carolyn smiled with approval as Maryellen's poodle skirt flared out in a perfect circle.

Just then, Carolyn's boyfriend, Doug, walked over. He didn't even seem to notice Maryellen. "Wow, Carolyn," he said. "You look gorgeous." Carolyn blushed, and the couple walked off holding hands.

Just when Maryellen was sure her sister had forgotten all about her, Carolyn turned and called back, "I promise I'll dance with you later, Ellie— if you're ready!"

The band began belting out their version of "We're Gonna Rock This Joint Tonight." To Maryellen, they didn't sound much like Bill Haley and His Comets, but they were good—and loud. She turned to the dancers and watched Joan and Jerry dazzle other onlookers with their fancy turns and flips.

"Wow," Davy said, coming up to join Maryellen.

"If you keep practicing like you did today, you'll be dancing like them in no time."

"No fancy flips for this pelican," Maryellen said. "I *am* ready to test my wings tonight, though, thanks to you." They grinned at each other, sharing their secret.

The drummer launched the band into the next song. Davy cocked his head, listening to the words. "Hear that, Ellie?" he asked. "It's 'Rock Around the Clock.' We sure did a lot of that the past couple of days."

The two shared a good laugh. They were just about to head off to the refreshment table when Carolyn stepped up. "Are you ready to rock 'n' roll, Ellie?" she asked. "Unless I'm cutting in," she said to Davy.

"No dancing for me, thank you," Davy said, putting up his hands. "Football's my game."

Davy was right, Maryellen thought. "Ready, Freddie," she said to Carolyn with a grin.

Maryellen joined the crowd of dancers, her heart fluttering as fast as the beat of the music. She followed Carolyn's steps—*to the right, to the left, to the back, to the front.* At the end, when Carolyn led her in a spin, Maryellen twirled faster than a spinning top and ended exactly where she was supposed to be.

"That was perfect!" Carolyn said. "You've got the steps down pat! How did you finally learn them?"

Maryellen felt a thrill at Carolyn's praise that rose all the way from her toes up to her cheeks. She looked at the band shell with its glowing lights and felt her face glowing, too.

"Let's just say I have a friend with Big Ideas," Maryellen said. She winked at Davy, and he winked back.

Inside Maryellen's World

In the 1950s, when Maryellen was a girl, rock 'n' roll was becoming popular. Inspired by this powerful new music—with amplified guitars, a thumping beat, and lively lyrics—teens invented fun dances like the twist, the pony, the slop, and the stroll. Teens loved rock 'n' roll dance parties, often called "sock hops" because party-goers slipped off their shoes to dance. By the late '50s, teens were snapping up records by musicians like Elvis Presley and flocking to rock 'n' roll movies.

Most movies in the '50s were made for teens. *Treasure Island* was different: It thrilled young moviegoers with an exciting story starring a young boy. The 1950 Disney movie was based on the novel *Treasure Island* by Robert Louis Stevenson, written in the 1880s. It tells the story of Jim Hawkins, an ordinary boy working in his mother's inn, who finds an old treasure map. He's drawn into a dramatic search for buried treasure on a tropical island and must outsmart a devious pirate, Long John Silver, before he can claim a chest full of sparkling gold coins.

More than a dozen movies and television shows have been made about *Treasure Island*. But, as Maryellen's story suggests, there are many real stories of sunken treasure, and many of these stories are every bit as dramatic.

In the 1950s, the invention of scuba gear allowed divers to breathe deep underwater, making searches for shipwrecks on the ocean bottom possible. Real-life treasure hunters were eager to explore the wrecks of Spanish and French ships that once plied the Florida coast. One treasure seeker, Mel Fisher, searched for nearly 30 years. Finally, in the 1980s, he found millions of dollars' worth of gold, silver, and jewelry that had been carried aboard the *Atocha*, a Spanish ship that sank during a hurricane in 1715. This discovery made Fisher and his family both rich and famous—they were featured in newspaper and magazine articles, TV shows, and even a movie.

While Fisher's story was amazing, the discovery of a sunken wooden figurehead, like the one in this story, would in many ways be even more remarkable. Unless it's quickly buried under mud at the bottom of the sea, wood disintegrates after only a few decades in the warm water of the tropics. Very few wooden remains from old ships have ever been found.

Still, modern-day treasure hunters continue to make exciting discoveries. In 2013, a Florida family searching for treasure found hundreds of thousands of dollars' worth of gold chains, coins, and a ring while diving just 150 yards offshore. It was part of a shipment of about $200 million in treasure that experts think still remains unclaimed on the ocean floor off Florida's coast. Who knows what might be discovered next?

Read more of MARYELLEN'S stories,

available from booksellers and at *americangirl.com*

✳ *Classics* ✳

Maryellen's classic series, now in two volumes:

Volume 1:
The One and Only

Maryellen wants to stand out—
but when she draws a cartoon of
her teacher, she also draws
unwanted attention. Still, her
drawing skills help her make a
new friend—with a girl her old
friends think of as an enemy!

Volume 2:
Taking Off

Maryellen's birthday party is a
huge hit! Excited by her fame,
she enters a science contest. But
can Maryellen invent a flying
machine *and* get her sister's
wedding off the ground?

✳ *Journey in Time* ✳

Travel back in time—and spend a few days with Maryellen!

The Sky's the Limit

Step into Maryellen's world of the 1950s! Go to a sock hop, or take
a road trip with the Larkin family all the way to Washington, D.C.
Choose your own path through this multiple-ending story.

✳ *Mysteries* ✳

Enjoy a thrilling adventure with Maryellen!

The Finders-Keepers Rule: A Maryellen Mystery

Maryellen finds a barnacle-encrusted ring buried in the sand
of Daytona Beach. Will it lead her to treasure—or trouble?

A Sneak Peek at

The Sky's the Limit

My Journey with Maryellen

Meet Maryellen and take a journey back in time
in a book that lets *you* decide what happens.

F lying, that's what it feels like. My skis skim across the top of the snow so smoothly it's as if I'm a bird swooping low over the ground. I'm all by myself, with blue sky above, white snow below, and me in the middle, flying down the mountain, as fast as a shooting star.

I'm not skiing for fun; I'm skiing to win a race, and skiing to win is very, very serious. I'd love to go where I want to go, choosing whichever trail looks freshest and fastest and most fun. But I have to stick strictly to the planned race route and follow it exactly as it is marked and try to ski perfectly to win for my team.

It wasn't my idea to be on the ski team and turn skiing into something tense and competitive. It was my twin sister Emma's idea. She loves to compete. She especially loves to win. And she just about always wins when the two of us disagree. Emma is not only my twin sister, she is my best friend, and I always want to make her happy. That's how I ended up on the ski team. Emma really, really wanted us

to do it together, so I gave in, as I usually do when
Emma has her heart set on anything.

A sudden burst of wind makes the powdery
snow swirl up all around me. The sun reflecting
off the snow blinds me just as the trail breaks into
two narrow branches. I squint, looking for a route
marker—a flag or an arrow—pointing to the branch
that I should take. But if there is a marker, it's hidden
by the whirling snow. Just then, someone waves, as
if signaling me toward the left branch, so I take it.
This branch of the trail winds through dense woods.
Then, as I burst out into the open, it sends me over
a huge mogul and I am airborne. That's fine with me.
I love jumps—the higher, the better! But it's risky and
unusual for a race route.

I zoom down the mountain, cross the finish line,
and pass the time clock, and—to my amazement—
I win the race.

I'm happy, though not as crazy excited as Emma
would be. Winning means more to her than it does

to me. I take off my gloves, skis, and goggles, and change my boots. I put on my eyeglasses and look for Emma as I hurry to the ski-race awards platform.

"Good job, Sophie! Way to go!" cheer my teammates. They gather around me and thump me on the back. Even Coach Stanislav is smiling for a change. In the crowd on the platform I see my proud parents and my grandmother. But where is Emma?

"Congratulations, Sophie," says the judge. She shakes my hand and gives me my prize.

"Whoa," I breathe. "Thanks." The prize is a fabulous vintage watch that's also a stopwatch. I take the beautiful watch out of its box, and I'm just strapping it onto my wrist when Emma appears.

"Sophie cheated," she says.

What?

"She took a shortcut," says Emma. "That's why she won."

"Emma, no!" I gasp. I plummet from happiness to humiliation in one second. How could she think

that I would cheat? She's my sister, my other half,
my twin. I know things have been a bit tense
between us ever since our grandmother came to live
with us and we've had to share a room. But is Emma
so mad that she'd lie about me? Does she really think
I cheated? I try to read Emma's face, but she won't
meet my eyes.

I'm not quick with words the way Emma is, and
now I struggle to explain. "I must have—I think
I made a mistake," I sputter. "I was blinded by the
sun, and I couldn't see any flag, and I thought someone pointed me down the trail, and—"

"Sophie!" Coach Stanislav interrupts. I'm not surprised; even to my own ears, my explanation sounds
weak. "If you cheated," my coach continues, "just be
honest about it."

"I *didn't* cheat," I insist. "I'd *never* cheat. It was an
honest mistake."

My mom slips her arm around my shoulders to comfort me.

"We'll have to look into what happened, Coach," says the judge. She turns to me and holds out her hand for the watch.

I undo the wrist strap with trembling, clumsy fingers. By mistake I touch the stopwatch button, and—*swoosh!*

Just for a second—

Just for the blink of an eye—

Just like when I was skiing—I have the sensation of flying, like a shooting star. And when it stops, I find myself . . . well, I'm not sure *where* I am.

I'm no longer on the ski mountain, that's for sure. Instead, I'm standing on a driveway by a small house. There's a station wagon in the driveway, along with a big silver camper trailer. A hot sun reflects off the trailer, and I realize that I'm roasting in my ski-team uniform.

The air is moist, and it smells nice, all fruity and

flowery. The driveway is bordered with palm trees, flowers, and large bushes heavy with—*lemons?* I touch one. Yup, it's a lemon.

Where am I? What has happened to me? It's obvious that I'm not in my snow-dusted hometown of Cedar Top, North Carolina, anymore.

I look at the watch, still in my hand. The last thing I did was accidentally press the stopwatch button. Could it possibly be the *watch* that transported me? If I press the button again, will it transport me home?

My heart quickens with hope. Maybe the watch will take me back to the moment on the trail before I chose the wrong route, before Emma's betrayal— before any of the bad stuff had happened yet.

But maybe the watch will transport me some- where else entirely. Then what?

There's only one way to find out.

I touch the watch button, and . . .

Swoosh! . . . Once again, I feel as if I'm flying . . .

When I open my eyes, I'm back on the awards

platform at the ski slope. Mom has her arm around me. Dad and Gran look sad. Coach Stanislav and the judge are frowning at me, and I can practically feel the chill waves of disapproval from all my team-mates. It's as if *no time at all* has passed, as if no one has so much as taken a breath.

If only I could prove that I did not cheat, that I just made a mistake. But how? Emma, who usually leads the way and often speaks for me, is my *accuser.*

I feel lost, hopeless, and overwhelmed. Suddenly, I just want to disappear.

Will the watch transport me again? I'd like to go back to the warm place, but I'd rather go *anywhere* than stay here. I love the stars, the moon, and the planets—I'd gladly go to another planet right now!

No one will miss me; they are frozen in the moment. And I need some time to figure out what to do about the ski race.

So, mustering all my bravery, I close my eyes and press the stopwatch button again.

Swoosh...

I'm swept up in the flying sensation... and when
I open my eyes, I'm back on the driveway, next to the
lemon bushes. I feel a warm rush of relief to be back
in this balmy, palmy place.

I'm admiring the camper trailer—it's as stream-
lined and silvery as a rocket ship—when the side
door of the house opens and a girl about my age
comes out.

She's skinny and cheerful-looking. Her reddish-
gold hair is in a bouncy ponytail that catches the
sunshine. A roly-poly dachshund waddles behind
her as well as two cute little boys—one is wearing a
fireman's hat—and a little girl wearing a tutu and
a cardboard crown.

I freeze, expecting suspicious questions about
who I am and what I'm doing in their driveway.

Instead, the ponytail girl smiles a friendly smile

and says, "Oh, hi! I'm Maryellen Larkin! Don't you just love the Airstream trailer? Everybody does. By the way, this is my sister Beverly. She's seven. The fireman is Tom, he's five, and the littlest guy is Mikey, who's three. Our dog is Scooter. We're so glad you're here!"

The littlest boy, Mikey, runs forward and flings his arms around my legs, practically knocking my eyeglasses off in the exuberance of his welcome.

Maryellen rattles on. "We've been excited ever since we heard that you were coming. You're going to love Daytona Beach."

Daytona Beach? Isn't that in Florida? I'm in *Florida*? And Maryellen and her family have been expecting me? I'm so flabbergasted that I'm breathless.

Tom, the boy in the fireman hat, asks, "What's your name?"

"Sophie," I manage to choke out.

I don't know why, but my name makes all the Larkins smile. I've never thought of my name or myself as a reason to smile before. It feels good,

I discover. I begin to relax a little.

"Sophie?" says Maryellen merrily. "Are you named after the singer Sophie Tucker? We see her on *The Ed Sullivan Show* a lot."

I shrug and grin. "I don't know," I say. I've never heard of Sophie Tucker or *The Ed Sullivan Show*. "Mom told me my grandmother thought up my name."

"My grandpop gave me the nickname Ellie," says Maryellen. Then she asks, "How old are you?"

"Ten," I answer.

"Me too!" says Maryellen.

"Do you have any brothers or sisters?" asks Beverly-with-the-crown.

I nod. "A sister," I say, tensing up a bit when I think of Emma.

"Mom's excited to meet you," says Maryellen. "Your Aunt Betty is one of her oldest friends."

"Betty visited us last year," Beverly cuts in.

"It was Mom's idea for you to come stay with us while Betty helps your parents move from New York to Washington, D.C." Maryellen starts to lead me toward the house. "It's lucky that Betty works for the airlines, so your ticket was free. Let's go inside. Mom can call your parents and tell them you're here."

"Uh..." I begin. I'm so confused and not sure what to say.

Just as Maryellen starts to open the screen door, Beverly stops her.

"Wait, Ellie," she says. "How do you know that Sophie is Betty's niece? Maybe she's a new girl who's moving into the neighborhood." Beverly turns to me and tilts her head. "Is that it?" she asks. "Are you and your family moving in?"

*✷ To go inside with Maryellen,
    turn to page 15.*

*✷ To agree with Beverly,
    turn to page 17.*

Author's Note

Special thanks for going the extra mile in assisting with information about Daytona Beach to Fayn LaVeille, Director of the Halifax Historical Society and Museum; Kim E. Dolce, Genealogy/Reference Librarian at the Daytona Beach Regional Library; and Eric Miller and Missy Phillips of the City of Daytona Beach Property Maintenance Dept.

About the Author

JACQUELINE DEMBAR GREENE is the author of the American Girl series about Rebecca Rubin. The books have won national awards, as have many of her picture books and historical novels. Ms. Greene has also written nonfiction books and several Rebecca mysteries. Besides writing, Ms. Greene loves to explore ancient areas that still hold secrets, such as the magnificent ruins and burial sites in Egypt and the tumbling pyramids in Mexico, Guatemala, and Honduras. Ms. Greene enjoys gardening, hiking, biking, and photographing the exotic places she visits.